ARCH GUARDIAN PUBLISHING

HOME OF THE FREELANCE AUTHOR

Mr Joe Louis Mitchell Jr

COPYRIGHT © 2018

TABLE OF CONTENTS

CHAPTER 1

A FLIGHT LIKE NO OTHER

It was a calm Tuesday the 11th of September, business as usual for a busy New York, New York day. Six O'clock A.M. no one around the country knew what that morning would bring. Nineteen hijackers would take control of four flights coming from Boston, Newark, and Washington, D.C. that was heading to San Francisco and Los Angeles.

Early that morning flight crew and passengers of American Airlines Flight 11 had no clue that this day would be their last. AA11 was to fly from Logan International Airport in Boston, Massachusetts to LAX in Los Angeles, California. It was clear skies and all was good to go to start a long flight to Los Angeles early that Tuesday morning.

The crew boarded the plane first to do their checklist to see if all was okay for their flight to take off. The captain and co-pilot checked all their flight instruments in the cockpit. All the cockpit instruments, engine instrument, navigational and communication equipment etc. seemed to work properly and there would be no problem for the flight to Los Angeles. The flight attendants checked the plane to see if all things were in proper and working order. They made sure they had all the things that were needed for the flight like meals and drinks carts. The ground crew loaded the passengers' baggage onto the plane.

No one knew that five terrorist hijackers were among

the passengers who were waiting to board the plane. There were 81 passengers waiting in the American Airlines waiting area for Flight 11. Seventy six of the eighty one passengers talk and joked around with each other before they were ready to be seated on the plane.

Then over the American Airlines loud speaker a voice said *"American Airlines Flight 11 is now ready to board first class passengers."* There were 9 first class seats on this Boeing 767-223ER and two of the five terrorist hijackers got in line to be seated in first class. After the first class passengers boarded the plane, a voice can over the AA loud speakers again saying *"now seating row 44 to 30."* So these passengers that were assigned to those seats boarded the plane one by one.

"Now seating passengers of Row 29 to 20", likewise as the first group, they did the same. The final call came over the loud speaker in the American Airline waiting room in Logan International Airport *"now calling row 17 to 4 of Flight 11 to board the plane."* These passengers joyfully walked onto the plane to begin their journey to Los Angeles, California.

As all the passengers and Flight Crew got settled down so the flight could take off. The pilot captain checked in with the airport tower to say they were ready. The aircraft was taxied away from gate B32 onto the airport runway around 7: 45 am Tuesday morning. Once the craft was taxied away from the gate the lead flight attendant began going over the correct aircraft procedures on what to do in case of an emergency, not knowing in a few minutes they would have a true life threatening emergency. The aircraft lined up on the runway, after the captain got the okay from the flight tower the plane moved down the runway strip. Picking up speed down the strip the pilot pull back on the aircraft controls and the plane began to get lift and take off the ground.

Now in flight the aircraft climbed to cruising attitude. Logan International Airport began to get smaller and smaller in the distance when the passengers looked out of the aircraft windows. The plane made its departure from the airport.

The ringleader of terrorist hijackers of American Airlines Flight 11 gave the sign to the other four hijackers that it was time to take control of the Boeing 767-223ER. The leader of the hijackers looked over to the other hijacker that was sitting in first class with him and nodded to say all was a go to take control of the plane. Likewise the other hijacker walked out of first class and give the signal to the other three that their plans were ready to be executed. They pulled out the weapons that they smuggled on the aircraft. The leader stabs one the passengers in first class in the chest. As he laid there bleeding to death, the lead hijacker yelled *"this is a hijacking, no one be a hero for we mean business"* as he grabs a flight attendant and holds a knife to her throat.

By this time all hell broke loose, the passengers were in an up roar. A passenger in the coach section of the plane tried to overtake one of the hijackers but as he jumped to tackle him the hijacker side stepped him and stabbed him in the back. The hijacker yelled ***"We told you'll don't be a hero and the next person who stands up we will kill!"***

The leader knocks on the cockpit door and demand to be let in; *"If you don't let us in the cockpit we will kill every last person of the flight crew."* So the aircraft captain fearing for the lives of his crew let the hijackers in the cockpit. The two hijackers that were sitting in first class walked in the cockpit and speared the pilot and co-pilot in the back with their knives. They threw the bodies of the two pilots out of the cockpit seats. They told the flight attendant that they took hostage that she could join the other three hijackers, *"you can go help the rest of the team control the passengers"* for she was in on the hijacking as well. They closed the cockpit door and locked it, because they had pilot experience they took control of the aircraft and flew it off course.

Meanwhile in coach a few of the passengers began to talk quietly among themselves. *"What is going on?"*

"Did they just kill someone in first class?"

"Don't talk so loud for we don't want them to come back here and try to harm us."

"We need to do something; we have no idea what they are planning to do."

"Yea but you heard what they said don't anyone try and be a hero." "I don't want to end up like that guy in first class that was stabbed for no reason!"

"I understand but if we don't do something we will all end up like that guy one way or another. I have a feeling this won't end good if we do nothing!"

As they had stop speaking the flight attendant who was taking hostage walked over to the three hijackers and said "we have hijacked the plane as planned."

In shock the other flight attendants couldn't believe what they just heard, "we have hijacked the plane as planned", wondering how she could have done this to them. Some of the passengers were thinking of how they could retake over the aircraft not knowing that the pilots were dead.

In the cockpit the hijackers made the aircraft change its course from Los Angeles unto New York City. The Leader of the hijacker who was sitting the co-pilot seat looked over at the other hijacker sitting the pilot seat and said, "Now we shall get our revenge on The United States of America."

One of the passengers that were in coach said to the others "I can't wait any longer; we need to do something and do something now! I believe we are not flying to LA any longer. And who knows where they are flying too or what they will do with us? For if we die I rather die fighting!"

Another passenger spoke up and said "you heard what they said no one try and be a hero. So why are you trying to get all of us killed? You don't know when they get to where they are going too that they just won't let us all go free."

"If they were going to let all of us go free why hijacked a plane with hostages? And if they just wanted to fly somewhere, why not just rent a plane and fly there? I feel they have some evil plans and it don't include us being alive when their plans are complete. So we need to do something now if we all want to stay alive! I will jump on one of the hijackers when he walks back here."

One of the three hijackers saw some of the passenger in the back of the plane talking to one another so he went to the back of the plane to stop them from talking. The passenger who wanted to attack the hijacker leaped out of his seat as the hijacker walked past him. He jumped onto his back, startled that someone had the guts to defy them he quickly reacted by throwing him to the floor and to make an example of him he stabbed him in the stomach with his knife. *"I told you all not to be any heroes, see what trying to be a hero gets you!"* The passenger was left lying in the floor of the aircraft bleeding.

"I told him not to try anything but he would not listen to me. All he did was get himself stabbed and has the hijackers real upset. Now he will bleed to death! Why did you have to try anything, I told you not too. Why didn't you just listen to me?"

The hijacker in the cockpit said to the other one, *"We are close to our target, just about 20 miles off from our strike."* They had planned on flying straight into The World Trade Center in New York City. And there wasn't a thing in their way to stop them from doing so. No one knew that the plane was hijacked or for that fact was off course and was flying directly into The World Trade Center North Tower. The Boeing 767 made a bee line directly to the North Tower. The aircraft was full of fuel and ready to make a hot mess of the North Tower.

Just before the aircraft connected with the North Tower there was a flash of light. A great explosion ignited when the plane flew into the side of the building. A huge and hot fire began to burn in the top half of the North Tower of the World Trade Center.

Around the same time as American Airlines Flight 11 was being hijacked so was United Airlines Flight 175, United Airlines Flight 93, and American Airlines Flight 77. Just as American Airlines Flight 11 crashed in the side of the North Tower the crowd on the street stood there in total shock. Wondering what have just happen, people began to yell *"a plane just flew into a building!"* *"That's the North Tower of the WTC and it was stuck by a big plane!"* The crowds flooded the streets of Lower Manhattan to see the black smoke come from the WTC North Tower cause by the fire that was burning uncontrollable.

Not moments after New Yorkers watched in horror the burning of the North Tower, United Airlines Flight 175 bolted like lighting into the WTC South Tower. Not one but both tower had been struck by airplanes before 9:30 A.M. Tuesday the 11th of September. The crowd was caught by surprise when the first tower was struck but when the second tower became victimized as the first the crowd was dumbfounded. Not knowing what to do they watched in fear. For a calm New York, New York day became as bad as anyone could have imagine Hell to be! But it got worse as the country learn that morning two other flights, United Airlines Flight 93, and American Airlines Flight 77 were also hijacker and crashed.

The country had no answers of why and who had done these hellacious deeds. As the twin towers collapsed and WTC 7 did the same, the people wonder who would pay for what they did that day that was like no other!

CHAPTER 2

BEGINNING TO KNOW

Some are born to be great while others have greatness thrust upon their shoulders. I guess when it comes to me, "Josiah Lewis" it would be a little of both. I was born in the small town of Hot Springs, South Dakota, apart of Fall River County. Who would have known that I become anything but a small town farmer. My parents ran a small dairy farm just outside of town. After school I had the usual farm boy chores. One day after school my mother said to me, *"Josiah do not forget to clean up the barn after you finish your homework!"* From that day on I knew I wanted more out of life than just being your average old farmer.

It wasn't that I did not like working hard at the farm because my parents raised me to work hard. The boredom of the farm that got to me. It was something about the action hero of the movies that I saw as a kid that I loved. Wishing to have an exciting life drove me to sports. To find a way out of being a small town farmer pushed me to be the best at whatever I did. My parents wanted the best for me and they knew I loved sports so they allowed me to play little league football, baseball, and track & field.

Being a born leader; I became team captain in each sport that I played. Though I played three sports football was the love of my heart. I played many positions on offense and defense in football but it wasn't until I got to play quarterback that I found the passion that I desired. Being able to lead a team down the field to score meant so much to me. Having the pressure on my shoulders made me realize I was destined to take charge.

My little league football coach would always say to me

"Josiah if we are to win I need you to play your best for our team follows your lead." I was the catalyst that lite the team on fire. Being the starting quarterback of the team, when I didn't perform well I let the team down.

One night after our little league practice some of my teammates and I were waiting on our parents to come and pick us up. We were just sitting around joking on each other. I would always make fun of Billy's pants. *"Billy why do you wear those high waters you don't live in a flood zone!"* For it was just silly jokes and we knew no one was serious so we never got mad at each other. So just sitting there joking I looked up in the sky and I saw three light. I thought it looked strange so I told the guys to look up. These lights moved in a weird way, first they sprung in a circular pattern. Then as they spanned around they began to move back and forth and side to side as if the lights were chasing each other. The guys and I was totally in awe for we just saw a UFO. I have heard of people seeing them but I have never seen one until then. What we saw that night we didn't know what to say or to do. So we promise to keep quiet about it, we didn't want people to think we were a bunch of crazy kids making up lies to just get attention. So we never told anyone what we saw that night, not even our parents.

High school was a fun time in my life. Like in little league, I played three sports in high school. Track & field helped me with my feet work in football; and baseball helped me improved my eye and hand coordination which made me a better quarterback. Every quarterback needs the ability of accuracy to help his team win the game. And winning the game was what matter to me for we play the game to win. I hated to lose, losing wasn't acceptable to me. People say it's doesn't matter if you win or lose, it's how you play the game. But if you play the game to win then it does matter if you win or lose! I refuse to lose. I believe in my abilities and if I use them no one can beat me.

It was the biggest game of my high school life; it was the South Dakota high school state class 11AA championship game.

My school "Buford High" vs. Oak Ridge High School was the battle of the unbeaten. Oak Ridge had the best defense in the state, for no team has score more than two touchdowns against them all season long. Their offense scored an average of 28 points a game. This was my senior year, the last game of my high school career and I didn't plan on going out as a loser.

It was a cold mid-November week. We had a challenge to prepare for the game because of the weather. The week of the big game our team Buford High Bobcats practiced harder than we have ever done before. Practicing for a championship game against an opponent that was one of the best at what they do would make many teams fear playing them. But I knew that our team wasn't a push over. We had one of the best passing offenses in the state. I had two top quality receivers and a very good running back with great hands. Our offense practiced against the first string defense to prepare each other for our opponent's attack.

"Go Bobcats Go" was the cheer that cried out at all our game. You could not miss the cheer when you came to the game; the cheerleaders always pumped us up with their many cheers. Hearing our cheerleaders cheer on the sideline during the game always pushed me to play harder. And this game would require our cheerleaders to bring some of their best ever. We needed all the support that we could get. Bring a 14 point underdog had people thinking we were going to lose.

I had waited all week for this Championship Game and this week felt like the slowest one of my whole life. Saturday morning I woke up around 8 A.M.. I wasn't able to sleep all night. I went over all the plays of the playbook in my head that night. I envisioned in my mind what plays the coach would call and me executing them to perfection. I saw myself in the huddle getting the plays from the coach and calling them out to the players in the huddle. "Red Dog Ace 17 Boot on 3", breaking the huddle after I called the play, I could see all of this in my head. This kept me up for hours Friday night and it was early Saturday morning before I could finally go to sleep. I even dreamed about throwing a touchdown to my number one receiver. This game consumed me all week long for I ate, slept and dreamed this game. For this week all that matter to me was this championship game.

Arriving at the championship game stadium early to get ready for our pregame warm ups and walk through. When I arrived I saw a huge crowd standing in line waiting to enter the stadium. If I had said that I wasn't nervous I would have been lying. It was the toughest challenge I had to face in my life up to that point. In every great athlete's career there is a defining moment that makes or breaks them. And this game would define me by the way I would perform. For if I perform poorly it would take me forever to shake it off. Colleges would remember the last game of my high school career. They would know if I could play under the pressure of the big game.

The whole team was in the locker room getting dress in our new football jerseys made just for this game. It was the school's first state championship game and that added more pressure to all of us. Oak Ridge High School was the two time defending class 11AA state champs. Buford High was in their way to make them the three-peat champion.

Now it was game time, we had gone over all our pregame game plans and warm ups. It was time for the rubber to meet the road. It was time to be known as a Champ or a Chump. I could hear our cheerleaders in the distance cheering, "Go Bobcats Go."

Oak Ridge won the coin toss and decided to receive the football first. Our kickoff team lined up to kick the ball to them. And the game was underway with a huge boom as our kicker's foot stuck the football. Our team ran down field to make a tackle, Oak Ridge player number twenty two caught the ball at their five yard line and made a few moves before our player number forty four made a huge tackle on their twenty nine yard line.

Now Oak Ridge started their first drive on their own twenty nine yard line. Their quarterback broke their huddle and brought their team to the line of scrimmage ready to execute the first play of the game. To our horror it was a seventy one yard bomb to their wide receiver number eighteen. It was like a nightmare, he ran ten yards and took two steps out toward the sidelines and turned up the field. I guess our cornerback thought he was performing an out route pattern for when number eighteen turned up field he left our cornerback in the dust. Their quarterback saw when his receiver turned that he was wide open so he threw a perfect ball. One of the best passes I seen thrown. He raced to the end zone for their first touchdown. They score too easily on one play. It had their crowd going crazy and our sideline was completely quiet and in total shock. We practiced all week to prevent this from happening.

They kicked the ball off to us and our number eighty eight caught the ball at the one. He ran up the middle, as he was hit he fumble the ball and their player number fifty six picked the ball up and walked into the end zone untouched for their second touchdown in 2 minutes. We were down two touchdowns now; the score was fourteen to zero. I couldn't believe what I was seeing. I ask our team. *"Did we not practice this week? Why were we playing like we were still in little league!"*

They kicked off for the second time and we got the ball to the twenty five yard line. It was my time to show Oak Ridge what we were made of. The coach gave me the play as I ran from the sideline. I called the play in the huddle, we broke the huddle and our offense lined up on the line of scrimmage. I called the cadence under center *"Set, Blue 42, Red 32, Blue 4, Hut, Hut, Hut"*, the ball was snapped and I tossed the ball to our runningback number twenty three on an off tackle toss. He run for thirty yard on our first play and our nerves were calm now for we got our first play out of the way. The next play the coach called a trick play called Hook the Sugar. It shocked me a little because it was early in the game but we were down fourteen to zero so we needed to get back in the game. I called the play in the huddle, *"Hook the Sugar on two"* I snapped the ball and our wide

19

receiver number eighty one ran down the field fifteen yards and turned around. I threw him the ball on a tight rope. He caught it with both hands, as he was catching the ball the runningback number twenty three was running toward him. So as he caught the ball he tossed it back to our runningback,who sprinted down the field for a TD. The first quarter ends with a score of fourteen to seven.

But before we knew it we were down thirty five to twenty with five minutes left in the fourth quarter. They had the ball and were trying to run the clock out to win the game. We needed two touchdowns and a two point conversion to tie the game up before the clock ran out. We needed our defense to make a stop or cause a turnover for it was under four minutes to go in the game. Just as I was thinking we need a turnover our linebacker number fifty six hit their runningback and made him drop the ball. One of our linemen fell on the ball. We had the football at mid-field.

The coach gave me the play, we broke the huddle. The play called for my favorite receiver to run a post route pattern. He lined up on the right side of line of scrimmage, I told him to come in motion toward the left side. As he got to the left side just outside the tightend I snapped the ball. He ran a deep post, ran twenty yard down field then ran a post at a forty five degree angle toward the back of the end zone. When he broke to the post I threw the ball off his back shoulder where only he could catch it. He went up in the air and grabbed it with one hand and came down with it in the end zone. It was one of the greatest catches I seen him make. The coach decided to go for a two point conversion. We ran a Halfback option. I snapped the ball and ran to the right side; just before their linebacker number forty five came to tackle me I tossed the ball back to our halfback number twenty three and he ran into the end zone for 2 points.

We were now down thirty five to twenty eight with three minutes left on the clock. We kicked the ball off for we believed our defense could stop them. Our offense had scored more on their defense than anyone has before. So we were very confident that we could beat them and win the championship. They had the ball on their on their thirty yard line and two and a half minutes left to play. They ran three plays and couldn't get ten yard for a first down. They had forth and four so they needed to punt the ball. The ball went out of bounds at our thirty five yard line. We had less than a minute before the end of the game. The play I dreamed of all night long the coach finally called.

"*Red Dog Ace 17 Boot*", I said in the huddle. We came to the line and I said "*Red 2, Red 2, Blue 18, Hut, Hut, Hut,*" and snapped the ball. I made a fake toss to the halfback and turned and ran a naked bootleg to the left. I saw nothing but open field for they bit on the fake. We had been running on them all game so they had to respect the run fake. It was a foot race, being on the track team help me with my speed. I felt like I could out run anyone to the end zone. I had sixty five yards to run and no one was going to stop me from reaching my goal of a touchdown. One tackler came at me and I made a spin move sprung out of his way while running full speed. I saw the end zone and dove across the goal-line.

We always believed that we play to win the game, so we decided to go for the two point conversion. We could have kicked the extra point and sent it into overtime but we wanted to win and win now. We knew that they would double team our best receiver number eighty one so our second best receiver had to be the hero of the day. I snapped the ball and number eighty eight made a fade to the back of the end zone and I threw the best pass I have ever thrown my whole life. I threw the ball on the tightest rope ever, I believed that it burned a hole through his hands but he was able to hold on to the ball and we score the two point conversion.

Now there was only twenty five seconds left in the game and we were winning thirty six to thirty five. We had to keep them from scoring a field goal and winning the game in the last seconds. We kicked the ball off and tackle the ball carrier at the twenty five yard line. Coach decided to put me in as a defensive back for we were running a dime defense. We ran a deep zone making sure no one ran pass us. They had the ball with only 2 downs to go for it was third and ten. The quarterback had a man deep so he threw it his direction but I read it all the way. Just before he could get it I ran over and grabbed it out of the air and had my first career interception.

We ran the remaining time off the clock. We did something no one had done in 2 years, score more than two touchdowns in a game against them and come from behind to win the game. We were the new Class 11AA State Champions. This moment would prove to be my defining one.

Having won the South Dakota Class 11AA State Championship it was now time to focus on my grades. It was my senior year, and I need a good GPA to get into a good college. There were many colleges and university who wanted to recruit me to play quarterback at their school. The University of Miami stood out for me because of their College of Engineering was where I wanted to study Aerospace Engineering. The University of Miami offered me a full football scholarship. Why did a farm boy want to major in aerospace engineering? I have always been intrigued by space ever since that day we saw that UFO. Being accepted to The U was a dream comes true. You could only have imagine four years in Miami, FL would be like for a Mid-West little town boy like myself. I graduated from Buford High with a 3.53 GPA. University of Miami here I come for 4 great years.

BIG MAN ON CAMPUS

I was a big fish in a small pond, now I was among 2000 new freshman on campus. It was a culture shock being at a big university away from home for the first time. Hot Spring, South Dakota was a microscopic town compared to Miami, Florida. Life apart from my parents seemed strange to me. Living in the dorm on campus had me missing the farm a little bit. I wonder how mom and dad were doing on the farm; I knew they missed me there helping them on the farm. I was the oldest of five kids. I have two younger sisters and two younger brothers. I was the first to leave home and go halfway across the country to go to college.

I was third on the quarterback depth chart. I was the new freshman quarterback so I needed to work myself up to the top of the pecking order. This was my first new challenge in college. I needed to prove to my new teammate and myself why The U recruited me to be here.

Majoring in Aerospace Engineering had me being double focus. Though football was my love, playing pro ball wasn't my dream. Football was a way to get to where I wanted to be. I dreamed about being an aerospace engineer. I have always wondered if there was life on other planets or designing a spacecraft that could take human beings to other planets.

There was a Senior and Junior quarterback on the depth chart above me. The senior quarterback has been the starter since his sophomore year. I was on the scout team my freshman year. I studied the ins and outs of the playbook. Because I was on the scout team the first year I didn't get to travel on away games. It gave me more time to study my class work when the team played games away. Aerospace course work wasn't something I could just fake myself through. I needed to really apply myself to study. I was focused both on my class work and on football. I was never the life of the party, though I like to have a social life I had better things to do than always being at a party.

Partying and chasing after girls would have kept me from reaching my goals. I refuse to lose, and not reaching my goals was not acceptable to me. Don't get me wrong I love a good party and a great looking girl like any guy but goals consumed me so they must be completed.

Twelve game seasons seemed so long riding the bench. I love getting on the field but I didn't step foot on the field to play one play that whole first year. I determined that last game of my freshmen year I would beat out all other quarterbacks on the roster to be the starter.

The summer after my freshman year I would work hard on becoming the starting sophomore quarterback. I ran the skill drills to work on my foot work, arm strength and accuracy. Being a backup wasn't for me. I needed the ball in my hands. I was a team player but I needed to be a leader. If I wasn't leading I wasn't doing what I was brought here to do. I didn't go home for the summer. I made sacrifices to reach the goals I had set for myself. I needed to stay at school and work out in the athletic facilities.

My first summer in Miami was a fun but hot time. Living in the north mid-west it never got as hot as it did in Miami. I had to learn how to get use to the heat. I understand now why the NBA team is called the Miami Heat for Miami totally has **HEAT!** The work outs were torture because of the heat. I believe I lost twenty pounds that summer. I became a lean mean quarterback machine, ready to compete for the starting job.

I ran plays and worked out with the second team offense to get myself ready to show the coaching staff what I could do. I had my work cut out for me to beat out the senior to be the starter. Too win the starting job; it wouldn't be the easiest thing to do by any means. The senior was a very good athlete and he had three years more of running the playbook than I did. But my will to success won me the job.

My first two season as the starter was good. But now I was the senior quarterback and I wanted to go out with a bang. I believe in leaving something better than when I started it. What that means to me is I always need to be improving myself. Each year I needed to be better than the year before. That held true for my grades as well. Since this was my last year at the university I needed to make a decision on what course I wanted my life to go in. I knew I didn't want to play pro ball, though football was a love of mines I didn't want to do it for the next ten or fifteen years.

On an away game to California I met a young man who was a fan of mines. I got to meet with him after the game. I met and talked to Albert Crown. He was a high school junior. He was kind of a jokester, laughing is his mission in life. Being the big man on campus he wanted to impress me with his many jaw dropping jokes. Albert loved the water and the talked about joining the Naval Academy after he was finish with high school. As I was talking to Albert it made me think when I graduated in the spring I would take my Aerospace engineering degree to the military. I just had to decide which branch of the military would work best for me.

I met a contact who was a recruiter from Quantico, Virginia that told me to consider Officer Candidates School of The US Marines. He said *"Josiah I believe you would be a great candidate for OCS. I believe you have what it take to be a Marine Officer son! Son you can be one of The Few, The Proud, The Marine!"*

I couldn't believe one meeting with Albert Crown had me considering joining the US Marines. I never thought about being a military man before that moment. It was said wisdom comes out from the mouths of babes. Not saying Albert was a baby but he was younger than I was and he help me get a little direction to my life at that moment of uncertainty.

I applied for OCS after I finished the season with The University of Miami. I believe being a well-known college football athlete help me get in to the program. I was the All-ACC, All-NCAA Quarterback three years running. I was a Heisman Trophy winner my senior year. I would be the first Heisman winner to join the US Marines the following year. Many people thought I was crazy to go to the Marines after winner that reward. They wanted me to enter the draft. Many pro football teams wanted to pick me out of the draft but that wasn't what I wanted out of life. I guess in a scent that The US Marines won the draft to get me.

I took two months to go home after graduation to spend some time with my family. It has been a long time since I was last home, for I was working hard at school for my grades and football. Mom and dad were so happy I came home for the summer to be with the family. They all really missed me and I likewise missed them. I hung out all summer long with my little brothers and sisters. I have almost forgotten what summer was like in Hot Spring, South Dakota.

After being in Miami four years the heat on a South Dakota dairy farm wasn't that bad. I told my family many stories about my life in Miami. Now that I was home I was happy to help around the farm for the family needed all the help I could give them. Times had been hard for them since I left to go to college. They were a hand short and had a lot of work to do. The last four summers had been about me and my goals. I didn't want to be the selfish son where it was all about me and what I wanted. My parents had sacrificed a lot to help me get to this point in my life. They never complained about me not coming home in the summer to help around the farm. They allowed me to be me, and I really loved them for that.

The summer was almost over and the time drew near for me to go to OCS in Quantico, Virginia. I spend my last few weeks working on the farm and working out to stay in shape for I knew OCS wouldn't be a piece of cake. The time has come for me to prove that I had what it took to be The Few, The Proud,The Marines!

FROM ONE OF THE
U TO THE FEW

Quantico, Virginia was the desired place to be for a man who wanted to prove he belong among the best of the best. Now that my summer break was over, I went to Officer Candidates School for the US Marines. I wanted to become a US Marine Officer and join the Marines Aerospace program. It was a career I looked forward to advancing in. Ever since that day that I saw the UFO as a kid, I have been intrigued by flight. But first I had to focus on OCS before I could ever get there.

OCS would prove to be the toughest 10 weeks of my whole life. It would take more than me just being athletic. Sports training were difficult but compared to OCS training it was a walk in the park. My Drill Sergeant was tough as nails. He knew how to break a man down. I saw him make a 6'5" 280 lbs. man cry. He said *"Solider The Marines isn't a place for babies, for if you going to cry you can just go running home to mommy and cry all over her shoulder while she wipe your tears!"* And that guy dropped out of OCS the next day and went home. Football came second nature to me, so I didn't really have to do much thinking for I always knew what to do before I had to do it. OCS was more of a mental challenge which had me thinking on my feet all the time. I needed to make split second decisions. Decisions that could mean life or death for the men I was leading. If I made the wrong decision, many of the men and women who followed me could die. That is a lot of pressure for a guy who trying to become a US Marine Officer. After a grueling 10 weeks of OCS I graduated top of my class to receive my commission in The US

Marine as a first lieutenant.

I join the US Marine Aerospace program after OCS graduation where I went to Aviation Preflight Indoctrination in Pensacola, FL for 6 weeks of training. Compare to OCS preflight school was a fun experience. All together my flight school training took me 77 weeks to complete with Aviation Preflight Indoctrination, Primary Flight Training and Advanced Flight Training. After 1.5 years of flight training I was a real US Marine pilot which was a dream come true. This boy who should only dream of flying since the night I saw an UFO has now become a man that was a Marine Officer pilot.

I joined the 2nd Marine Aircraft Wing after I completed flight training. My unit was Marine Aircraft Group 31 (MAG-31) which I pilot an F/A 18 Hornet. I flew a tour in the first Gulf war where I saw a lot of action.

After the gulf war Operation Desert Storm I was promoted in rank to Captain. My post war primary mission of my fighter was air defense. I flew my F/A 18 to protect the country of air attacks from our enemies. There were things I saw that I would have never thought I would have ever seen. When I was a kid I could not imagine flying a supersonic jet beyond the speed of sound. To be moving so fast that you see an object way before you hear the object would have blown my mind as a kid. The first time I broke the sound barrier flying the F/A 18, I could have wet my pants. The boom it made when I reached the speed of Mach 1 sent chills up and down my body. I have never felt anything like that moment before in my life. To have the power in my hands, all of that under my control was an extreme thrill that nothing else could match.

One day I was flying routine air defense missions I saw something that I haven't seen since I was a kid. I called to base and said *"Squadron 224 Captain Lewis to base."*

Base controls responded *"Base here go head Squadron 224."*

"Base I am seeing 2 unidentified bogeys."

"Squadron 224 we need you to try to identified it."

"10/4 Base Squadron 224 out."

I saw two unfamiliar objects in the sky that I haven't seen before. The objects weren't aircrafts. I saw them in the distance and on my jet radar system. I put on my afterburners to catch up with the objects. As I caught up I began a chase so a dogfight was underway. The UFOs were flipping and turning trying to out run my jet. I was keeping up as best as I could. But my F/A 18 was no match for this unfamiliar aircrafts. I tried to keep up as they flipped I flipped chasing them across the sky. They moved back and forth in the sky like no aircrafts that I have ever seen. With all my years of flight training no craft has moved this way. Then like a flash of light they were gone. Not believing what I saw I return to base to file a report on what I saw up there. As I explain to my superior officers what I saw it seem too crazy to be real. So the official report read the object was an air weather balloon that has gone off course. But I knew the truth of what I saw, for it wasn't a weather balloon.

I kept in touch with Albert Crown over the years since that game I played in Cali where I first met him. After Albert finished high school he joined the Navy. He has always a lover of the sea. A surf head from the start, so Albert was destine to join the Naval Academy.

When I was going through my flight training Albert has just enter into the Naval Academy. We began to bond, and would keep in touch at less once a month to find out what each other was up too. After Albert's graduation from the Academy which he finished at the top of his class, he was station on an aircraft carrier in the Mediterranean Sea not too far from Greece.

A few years after the Gulf War when Albert was station in the middle of the Mediterranean my Marines unit began a three month training tour on his aircraft carrier. It was the first time I have met up with him in years. He was as lively as a joker as I had remembered him to be. When we had our down time after our training sessions, Albert would pull pranks on his crew and mines alike. It did not matter who the person was long as the person was of a lower ranking class than him. But when it was time to be serious he was very focus. Albert believed in if you work hard you need to play even harder to keep things balanced.

I was a hard worker but didn't have the play hard thing down too good until I got around Albert. He was a great friend for me to be around to help me stay balance, for my fun and serious meter would swing all the way to the serious side and never make its way back to the fun side. With Albert loving to crack a good joke I was able to find my balance.

During my unit's three month tour on Albert's carrier, Al told me of some of the strange stuff he has seen at sea. One night while making his rounds on the deck Albert said he saw strange lights in the distance. They moved in a way that a modern aircraft couldn't. He called down to the aircraft radar room about the lights he saw. But they told him that the radar didn't show anything. The radar screen was clear. The object that Albert saw was unidentified for he was the only one that saw it. When I told him I had a similar experience. I chased some unidentified bogeys only months before he saw those strange lights that moved like a strange ship in the night sky.

The newly appointed top secret agency General Alien Services code name (G.A.S) came to me to make me their new top special agent. They let me pick my own partner. Albert having some of the similar extra ordinary experiences, I didn't see a better candidate to be my partner in the new UFO agency. So I chose Albert Crown.

CHAPTER 3

NO LONGER PARADISE

Many light years from earth there's an alien planet called Varldoion. Varldoion is in the solar system of Jodajoton. Jodajoton is in a faraway galaxy, which is about 200 light years from Earth. The planet is inhabited by 4 billion strange beings.

The Varldoionains are one people. They have a bond and unity not seen on Earth. The Varldoionains have learned to work together in harmony that governs everyone equally. Varldoionains are rational beings who like thinking things out fully, rather than relying on their emotions.

Varldoion is governed by the Varldoionain Royal Council. 200 Varldoionains sits on the Royal Council. Every 14.3 Varldoion years, which is 10 earth years, The Varldoionains select new Royal Council Members so the balance of power stays equal.

Varldoion was a peaceful planet until something changed the course of their lives forever. A warm paradise could best describe how Varldoion was before the planet became less than paradise. Being the sixth planet in their solar system, which has 11 planets, it was too far from their star too sustained live. One billion years ago Varldoion developed its own heating source which made the planet suitable for life. In recent times the planet's life source began to go out.

Over the last two hundred years Varldoion dropped one degree a year of its average temperature. On average Varldoion's paradise temperature was eighty five degrees. The average temperature has become -115 below zero and is continuing to drop each year.

As the planet got colder, the Royal Council devised plans to deal with the situation. They began to build buildings that were better suited for the changing weather temperature. With all their advance technology they could not figure out what cause the change in temperature. Neither could they figure out how to stop the change. Quickly with each passing year their planet was drawing closer to an ice age.

Their planet being almost completely iced over, the atmosphere became unsuitable for live. Adapting their building to the change in the atmosphere were not enough to help them survive. When the temperature down to the point where verbal communication became very difficult, being a adapting specie they developed empath capabilities. They developed the ability to talk to each other through their thoughts. As they got more skillful in this ability, they were able to read the minds of lesser life forms. They could make lesser life forms see anything they wanted them to see.

The Varldoion Royal Council decided that it was time for drastic action. They could no longer live on their planet. Though the thought of leaving their planet was so very unthought-of, but living on a planet that has begun an ice age was not an option. The council met to devise a plan that would be the survival of their race.

The council decided to develop temporary technology space shelters that would orbit their planet. Having to build temporary technology space shelters for 4 billion beings was an extreme mass effort. The council knew the shelters would not last long with the growth of their race.

So the Royal Council called upon one the captains of their Royal Guards to lead a search party to discover a new suitable planet for their race to inhabit. So they called upon Ploutcraft and charged him with the orders of discovering their new planetary home. Ploutcraft could choose any of the Royal

Guards that he wanted and needed to complete his search party mission. The Royal Council told him to choose any equipment and supply that was need for the mission. A part of Ploutcraft search party was Larker, his mate and 1st Officer of his Royal Guards. Ploutcraft take 50 Royal Guards in his search party which includes his mate Larker and 2nd officer B'Elanna Linkasa who was female in gender.

Ploutcraft mind control ability enable him to make lesser beings see him as anything he want them to see him as. Ploutcraft true appearance is tall and slender having a shiny milky white skin. Ploutcraft has a long slender oval shape head with long straight navy blue hair. His nose is long and straight. He has a mouth that is medium in size with thin black lips. His teeth are sharp and pointy as shark teeth. He has a long slender neck. He has two eyes that are a solid baby blue color. Ploutcraft walks upright on two legs. His arms are long with human like hands. He wears a two piece Varldoion Royal Guard spacesuit that is twilight lavender and black with a Varldoion Captain Royal Guard symbol. The boots are black. Away from their planet Varldoion, they are able to learn and speak other languages quickly

Ploutcraft chose the starship Varldoion Sho'aunor'es which translates to [Varldoion Source Of Power] to complete the mission. They have developed some alien technologies that people on Earth have never dreamed of. They have developed a mood of travel that can get them from point A to point B which could be light years apart in a blink of an eye. Their ships can open up warm wholes from anywhere in the universe to any set location in a moment's time.

Larker of The Varldoion Royal Guard age in Earth years is unknown. 1st Officer Larker is the 2nd in command of the starship Varldoion Sho'aunor'es. Larker shares a passion with Ploutcraft that is unknown among the Varldoionain People. It's almost like a human emotional love, which the Varldoionains don't express. How the two of them developed these emotions is unsure, but they are a couple that co-exist together to run a discipline crew. Larker makes sure that Ploutcraft orders are follow out to the tee. She supports his no matter what he decides to do. Varldoionains are rational beings who like thinking things out fully, rather than relying on their emotions. Larker and Ploutcraft bond has seemed to change that for them. They are two of a kind, being apart from each other could cause them to come very irrational.

Larker's appearance is very similar to Ploutcraft but she looks very feminine. Her skin texture is similar to Ploutcraft; she has long wavy style hair that's as red as fire which goes the entire way down her back. Her eyes are a solid bright emerald color. Her lips are the same color of her hair. Larker wears a Female Varldoion 1st Officer Royal Guard Dress that is Onyx and Jade in color with matching Onyx boots. Her outfit has a 1st Officer Royal Guard symbol on it.

Ploutcraft having selected all of the crew members that he calculated was needed for the mission checked the ship supplies log to see if the starship was stocked with the needed supplies. Having the dire need of the mission being a success there wasn't a supply that was of a more important nature than the other. Ploutcraft not knowing what or who they would face on the search of their new planet loaded many high tech weapons on their starship. His specie had a high protein diet. Their food source was an alien tech generated meat substance that resemble meat but wasn't really meat. It had all the protein, vitamin and mineral that they needed to survive.

Ploutcraft, Larker, B'Elanna Linkasa and the rest of his Royal Guard crew boarded Varldoion Sho'aunor'es. Varldoion Sho'aunor'es was a large strange looking starship. Normally this ship held 250 crew members, but 50 crew members could operate the ship properly leaving more room for extra supplies. There were three big circular ship bases that were connected by three long connection arms that have the starship to form a triangle shape. In the center of the triangle shape starship was a small circular bridge where the ships operation was held. The bridge set up high in the center and three smaller connection arms extended down to connect one to each base.

Ploutcraft ship's computer has found a suitable inhabitable planet in Earth. Ploutcraft's 2nd Officer B'Elanna Linkasa puts the location of Earth into the ship's destination computer and set a course to Earth. Ploutcraft mission is to explore Earth and report back to the Varldoion Royal .

Counsel on its inhabitability. The ship had open up a worm hole to travel just outside of Earth orbit atmosphere. When traveling through space the starship spins in a circular motion with the bridge staying stationary while the entire ship span. From a distance each ship base and bridge seem to be its own starship, for the connection arms cannot be seen.

In each circular base are surface transporter ships. Small search party would leave the mother starship Varldoion Sho'aunor'es and travel to surface of the planet to explore Earth. Ploutcraft took 19 crew members including Larker and B'Elanna Linkasa with him in the transporter ship to explore Earth. Strangely enough this isn't the first time that Ploutcraft specie has visit Earth. In exploring the universe the Varldoion for 1000s of years has traveled to Earth to find out what Earth had to offer. But this time there visit would be totally different. Not looking at Earth's resources but Earth itself so that it could be their new home.

GAS IS MORE THAN
A RESOURCE

On Capitol Hill, Washington, D.C. the government formed a new top secret government agency. For years the US government knew of the present of space alien. Though publicly the US government denies the reality of UFOs but privately admit that they do exist. The government thought it was against national security for the public to know the realism of UFOs. Top government security officials met on Capitol Hill to talk about what would be done about UFOs and how they could keep it a secret from the public.

They needed a secret way to fund this agency that would take control of the space alien's conflict. The officials devised a plan to add higher taxes on the gas prices, with 100s of millions of people buying gas in the US each day the collection of these taxes could fund the agency each year three times over secretly. To explain the gas price increase the government would claim that the price of oil has increase. The government secretly in control of Wall Street made them to have it look like that oil prices has really raised but the true reality was nothing has changed.

They named this agency G.A.S code name standing for General Alien Services. A top secret base was needed for G.A.S. Government architects design this base beneath the remote Texas plateaus. The base was named GAS 225. They designed GAS 225 to be located near a small college town called Brentwood. Being about 150 miles due west of Brentwood, Texas, the base entrance was designed to look like an old run down 1950's style gas station.

The agency made an older gentleman name Nicky Jones that seen to be senile the guardian of its entrance. Nicky was an alien that crashed in Roswell, NM in the early 1950's. The US government ran test on him and brain washed him to have him forget he was an extraterrestrial being. They altered his appearance to make him look more human. The brain washing caused Nicky's mind to stay in the 1950's which the government used the design G.A.S's entrance to keep Nicky thinking that he was still in the 50's. Nicky Jones being the gas station attendant of the G.A.S base entrance believes that he works at a gas station in the 1950's. He has lost his scents of time; his reality is based in fantasy. G.A.S has made Nicky to run the fake gas station that never has a customer. Nicky believed that the G.A.S Agents are the gas station customers. Each time that Nicky sees an agent he thinks it's a different customer.

The government officials discussed which military officials they would seek to run G.A.S. They chose retired Major General Nicole Beck as G.A.S UFO Agency Department Head whose background was in Army administration. Nicole brought her former assistant Major Angela Edwards that she trusted. The agency need for scientists so they hire James Johnston and Tom Strathmore two of the best military scientist in the country. Then they chose one of the top US Marine Officers Captain Josiah Lewis, who was a pilot, to be a G.A.S UFO Special Agent. G.A.S had allowed Josiah to choose his special agent partner. It was important to G.A.S all assistants be a person that an agent could trust that their secret would stay a secret. So all agent were allow to choose military personnel that they could trust. Josiah chose the only person he felt he had a connection with, so he chose Lieutenant Junior Grade Albert Crown. Albert being a decorated officer of the Navy has moved up in rank quickly made him a great match for Captain Josiah Lewis partner.

The last agent chosen by Nicole was Special Agent Awesome Blossum as G.A.S species sketch artist. Agent Blossum has her background in military weapon sketch design. Nicole met Awesome Blossum while she worked for an Army weapon contract company. Nicole knowing G.A.S needed an agent to draw sketches of alien species so the agency could keep a record of all known alien she felt there was no better candidate than Awesome.

Because the agency was top secret all agents needed a cover story life. All agents were required to live in Brentwood to have the appearance of a normal life. G.A.S helped all agents to acquire their background cover story; some were made up while most used their military background to come up with their cover story.

After being contacted by G.A.S to join their agency Josiah Lewis accepted the new opportunity for a career change. Receiving his honorable discharge from the US Marine Captain Josiah move to Brentwood, TX to obtain is briefing of his new life. G.A.S has arranged for him to work at Brentwood State University as a part-time aerospace professor to be his cover. Having a high profile from college and the military G.A.S used his present past as retired US Marine Officer that became a small college professor. Josiah loved the fact he became a UFO secret agent that was pretending to be a college professor. He never dreamed as a little kid that the opportunity of an UFO agent would come knocking on his door. To him it's like a fantasy, a dream that he never wants to wake up from.

Albert Crown moved to Brentwood after receiving his early honorable discharge from the US Navy. G.A.S helped Albert purchased a night comedy club so his cover story would be a retired Navy Officer owning a club. Being Josiah special agent partner Albert story has the appearance that he moved near Josiah because they are best friends. So Albert and Josiah hung out a lot on duty and off duty to keep up appearances.

Major General Nicole Beck and Major Angela Edwards were retired Army Officials. G.A.S based their cover story on the fact that they were close friends so they decided to enjoy their retirement together in a small slow pace town. They were around the same age and being single with all their children grown they moved in a large house that they bought together.

A simple small town life for two top military scientists would seem a little out of the ordinary so G.A.S had to completely make up a life for the scientists. G.A.S changed their name so no one would have known who they were before they came to Brentwood. Tom Strathmore and James Johnston were given totally new identities, new names and lives in Brentwood, Texas. For whom they were before arriving to town no one will ever know and it will remain a mystery. G.A.S helped Tom and James get jobs at Brentwood State University as Professors of Chemistry. G.A.S made up Tom and James background as MIT grads that taught chemistry at a few different small Texas state colleges over the past decade.

Brentwood population is about 6000 people, which is one of those small towns where everyone knows each other. To hide a secret in plain sight in a town where everyone knows your secret will take skills and precision which G.A.S was up to the challenge. One slip up and G.A.S would make front page news all around the nation about their existence.

CHAPTER 4

THE LOVE OF A SMALL TOWN

My arrival at the new government department G.A.S was a fun day. I went from Captain Josiah Lewis to Special Agent Lewis which no one was allowed to know who I really was. The official report of my discharged was I retired from the US Marines to go teach at a small town college. Behind the scenes G.A.S pulled their government stings to get me the job teaching Aerospace science at Brentwood State University. It was a part-time gig which I taught twice a week for about an hour.

Being undercover was different for me; I was never the one to pretend to be something I wasn't. But when this opportunity as a UFO agent knocked on my door I was willing to do what it took to be a success in G.A.S. If it took me retiring from the Marines and pretending to be a college professor I would do just that!

Growing up on a small farm town I understood what it would take to live in a small college town. I missed the small town when I went to the big university. The big city was always jumping with things to do and parties to go too. Being a small town boy it has always been my first love.

After getting settled in with G.A.S I drove the SUV, which G.A.S appointed to my care, to Brentwood to spy out the town. Once I arrive in town I will need to find a place to live. I want to get settle down before I have to teach my class at BSU in four weeks. Brentwood is only 30 square miles or 19199.9 acres in size, which means there isn't much to do.

Albert has brought a little life to town with his new comedy club. It will become the new watering hole where you will see many of the town folks. Comedy fits Albert well. I never knew he could do stand-up though he is a wild and crazy guy.

I went to the nearest real estate agency to see about purchasing a house that I could live in. Having saved my money when I was in the Marines and having a retirement fund I was kind of well off. I could afford a nice house in a nice neighborhood. It was a nice Monday afternoon when I got to an agency called First Brentwood Real Estate. Though it was called first I believed it was the only real estate business in town.

A middle age gentleman greeted me at the door. *"Welcome sir, come in and have a sit. I get one of our skillful agents to help you."* Which I responded by saying *"Thank you sir, I would like that very much."* I guess I set there about five minutes and a lady walked over to greet me. She said *"Hello my name is Janet Walker, how may I help you today?"* I said to her *"Hi my name is Josiah Lewis; I am new in town and starting a new job at BSU in a few weeks. I am looking to purchase a house and I saw your business and decided to come in for your help."*

"Mr. Lewis we can definitely help you in this matter! Is there anything particular that you had in mind?"

"Ms. Walker I was looking for a nice size house in a good quiet neighborhood. Other than that I am not really sure."

"It's okay we can help you look around to see what you like. What market price is in your range? Do have a family or will you be living alone?"

"I'll be living alone. I don't have a family; my military career was my focus. Who knows if I meet the right woman I might think about settling down but as of right now I'm not looking to settle down. As for my market price range I'm looking in the 200k – 300k range. Not having a family while I was in the military help me be able to save money so I could have a nice sum when I retired plus my mili-

tary pension and my professor job has me well off."

"Okay Mr. Lewis knowing what you are looking for and your price range helps us find your new home. There a community on the west side of town that sounds like what you are looking for. We have some new houses that just have been built in the Westchester Heights Community. If you have some time now we can drive over there and have a look at them to see if you see anything that you like."

"Ms. Walker I believe there is no better time than the present, so I am free to take a look."

We decided to drive across town to this newly built community. It was a nice and quiet subdivision. Normally the homes in Westchester Heights would run in the 500k to 700k range in most subdivision around the country. We arrived at Westchester around 5 O'clock in the afternoon, and the sun was shining bright as it did for that time of the day. We had at least 3 to 4 more hours of daylight because it was a mid-summer day. We drove up to this beautiful Colonial style Spanish Eclectic house. It was a big two story home that fell into my price range. The construction on this house was finished four month ago and no one seemed to want to put a contact on it. I believe the house gods had it waiting for me to come and buy it.

My mouth dropped open when I saw this house. The Navajo white stucco exterior caught my eye when we drove up to the house. There was a round tower on each side of the house. It made this house look like a castle fit for a king. It had a low pitched roof with red tile roof covering and the eaves had little overhang. There were arches above the doors and windows, the upper story included a wood balcony. The exterior of the house was breath taking. The house had an asymmetrical design. The house was only seven months old and hasn't been purchase. I never thought I could get a house like this in my price range. The asking price was in the mid 250k.

The interior had to be as beautiful as the exterior. As we pulled up the driveway the landscape was in perfect condition. I only dreamed of grass being so green, and wonderful trimmed hedges. The gardener must have had a green thumb to get the whole yard looking like it was a Garden of Eden. I told Janet depending on what the interior of this house is like I may not need to see another house, for the landscape and the exterior has grabbed my heart.

As we walked through the front door my mouth dropped again, the large ceiling of the foyer that led to the living room. The living room alone seemed to be too much to believe. This house has sat here for seven mouths and no one had wanted it. This four bedroom house was complete with a large living room, den, dining room, large kitchen, three and half bathrooms and an office, which included a completed basement.

"Ms. Walker I love what I see, the neighborhood is for me. It seems so peaceful here. The house is what I am looking for; the completed basement has sealed the deal for me. I would like to put an offer of $245,000 in cash on the house and will pay all closing fees."

"Mr. Lewis you can call me Janet. I knew when you saw this house you was going to love it. It has been on the market for a little while but the right person just haven't come around until now. I will give the owner your offer. I will get back with you and let you know what the owner says about your offer."

"Thank you Janet for all your help, and I look forward to hearing from you."

"Josiah, you are very welcome, and it has been a pleasure meeting you today. You will hear from me soon. May the rest of your day be good."

I left the house thinking Janet Walker was a nice real estate salesperson who knew my taste of style. She only needed to show me one house. No need to showing many houses when she knew the one I would want.

As I pulled out of the driveway a thought came to me, I love the feel of a small town. Brentwood had me a little home sick of Hot Springs South Dakota. I was wondering how mom and dad were doing on the farm back home. I couldn't tell them the whole truth about why I really moved to Brentwood, Texas. I told my family the half-truth that I was retiring from The US Marines and I accepted a part-time professor position at Brentwood State University in Brentwood. No one was allowed to know the truth of me being a UFO Special Agent. I had this thrilling life that no one could know about.

This small town didn't have many hotels a guy could choose from, but the most descent one was good enough for me until I purchased the house I was looking for. So I drove back to the hotel to get a good night sleep. I had to report to work first thing in the morning, 0600 hours, to the G.A.S base GAS 225 for more briefing. I wasn't the type to be late. I arrived at the hotel around 1900 hours so I figure I would order some room service to get me something to eat before I settle down to bed at 2100 hours. I thought I would watch a good action movie on TV while I eat my dinner. The funny thing about the movie was it was a shoot 'em up flick where the star is a guy that is a gun crazy cowboy who shoots first and never asks any questions. This cowboy was a wild guy and his love of guns matched his love to shoot them. This type hero I never imagine myself being, I have always been careful how I used a firearm.

My alarm clock went off early at 4:30 in the morning, though I was a retired US Marine I still kept my shower, shave, and dress routine in 30 minutes or less. Dressed in my civilian attire, which was strange to me for the last twenty years I dressed in my Marine officer's uniform, I was out the door by 0500 hours. I had to make a quick stop to pick up my partner Albert Crown at his place. When I arrive at Albert's place he was ready to go. So we left his place at 0515 hours and had 45 minutes to travel 150 mile. Normally this wouldn't be impossible but because no road leads to the base my agent assign SUV was design to do more than drive. The SUV has the ability to fly, I was glad to be a retired pilot, so we arrived at the base with 15 minutes to spare. Just a quarter mile from the base is a runway so the agent's vehicles can land and drive up to the base entrance.

Nicky Jones mans the 1950's style gas station. As we drove up to the base Nicky was at the station so we pulled up to the gas pump to pretend like we was a customer of Nicky's gas station. We did this so we wouldn't blow our cover to Nicky Jones. The government has been in control of his since 1953, they had been running test on him. When they formed G.A.S they charged us to watch over him. So G.A.S made him to believe he was managing a gas station in the 50's. Since his mind was lost in time it was our orders as UFO Agents to make sure his mind stayed lost in time. It wasn't an order I agreed with, in my military career there were many orders given to me by my commanding officers I didn't agree with but I was trained to follow them.

We pulled into the gas station garage and as the garage door closed an elevator lowed us to GAS 225 base. When the elevator reached the lower level of the base parking area I parked the SUV. Albert and I walked to our office and waited there for the special agent's meeting to begin. As we were waiting for the briefing the department head walked in to our office to greet Albert and me for the first time. Nicole Beck was a highly respected Army general who has now been appoint to run G.A.S. She been in town for two months making sure that all the ins and outs of G.A.S has been taking care of.

"Good morning Agent Crown and Agent Lewis I am Director Nicole Beck, it's great to finally meet you both. I have heard some good things of the both of y'all. We will be meeting here shortly with all the G.A.S special agents to go over the department policies and procedures. After our meeting today Assistant Director Angela Edwards will run a tour of the base so that everyone is more familiar with everything."

"Director Beck Agent Crown and I are happy to be a part of G.A.S. I want to thank you for giving us the opportunity to be a part the team."

"Yes Director Beck we are happy to be here, being a UFO Spe-

cial Agent is like a dream come true for this old navy officer. I know Agent Lewis and I will do the best we can do as G.A.S agents."

The department policy and procedures meeting began not long after we met Director Beck. She introduced to us Assistant Director Angela Edwards. She was her right hand lady. Director Beck ran our briefing; she told us what G.A.S expected of all of us. We were to keep G.A.S a secret. No one and she meant no one could ever know G.A.S exist. It was everyone's responsibility to keep G.A.S as a top secret. The knowledge of the existence of aliens was of national security and the public were to never know. G.A.S agents were to protect the public from aliens in the shadows.

As far the public knew all alien sightings would be call the war on terror. G.A.S responsibility would to be to put a spin on everything concerned alien to be called terrorism that the public would not know the truth about aliens. Director Beck explained to us if you tell a lie to the public long enough this lie becomes truth to the public. If you write the lie down in the history books to the public the lie becomes true facts. The government has been doing this to the public for hundreds of years and will continue to do so. Nicole said that government set down these procedures for the agency to follow and G.A.S must follow them to the tee. And by any means necessary the real truth must be hidden. The briefing ended by Director Beck welcoming all personnel to G.A.S for we had some great things which we were called to do for our country. It sounded like the speech I received when I joined the US Marines.

Assistant Director Edwards gave us the tour of GAS 225. It was a secure fortress. There were nothing known to man that could breach its security. The security system was the state of art. Retina and palm scanners, laser motion sensor were just some the security figures of GAS 225. We walked over to the science lab where Tom Strathmore and James Johnston were in charged. They are the lead scientist whose responsibilities were to come up with new G.A.S tech for field agent. When dealing with aliens we needed a special tech to complete with alien technology. The lab scientists create many tool and weapon technologies every day that we the G.A.S agents relay on.

I was surprised to see the Tosba Calvary-Cross, which became a popular SUV in American, with the ability of flight. Billionaire James Tosba developed his brand of automobiles in the mid 50's and became very popular in the midland and west United States. I have flown many types of aircrafts in my military career and the Calvary-Cross handles as well as many of them. G.A.S scientists took an ordinary Tosba automobile and modified it to have flight and war battle abilities. CC would transform into fighter jet with a push of a button. The SUV front grill modifies into pointy jet nose for flight. Wings extend from the base of the SUV and the wheels flatten, jet exhaust extends from the SUV back hatch door. The SUV back spoiler would modify into a jet tail wing. Though Calvary-Cross flight speed wasn't as fast as my F/A 18 Hornet but was faster than a two seater plane.

Touring the science lab was an exciting experience. Seeing all the new gadgets actually gave me goose bumps. After seeing the science lab we concluded the briefing so we could call it a day. As we closed our briefing I asked Director Beck a question. *"Is there a gadget device we can use to help us hide the present of alien life forms on the planet from the public?"*

She answered me and said, *"The most cost effective way to hide this from the public is the lie campaign. You reach a mass public, and you tell them what you want them to believe and no gadget needed."* I didn't believe in spreading lies, but being a military man I understand protecting National Security. So I tolerated a little justified evil for a greater good. So the good result out weights the evil that cause the good. That was how I had to look at it, for my parents raised me not to go around telling lies. I took it as a superhero hiding his identity of who he really is to protect the ones he loves. It was all about the GREATER GOOD! We need to protect the public from themselves. If the public knew what we know the chaos would be insurmountable. There would be groups of crazies in every city around the nation doing unthinkable acts because of the fear of aliens.

The day's briefing was over, for it has been a long day so I told Albert I was ready to call it a day and he agreed with me. We loaded up in the Calvary-Cross and headed to the elevator to go back up to the gas station garage. We drove out of the garage and waved at Nicky to say thank you for the service, and Nicky waved back and said *"Y'all come back and visit us again soon!"*

As we drove off from the GAS 225 my cell phone beeped for I had a message from Ms. Janet Walker. For my personal cell phone doesn't receive service in GAS 225. Ms. Walker unable to reach me left me a message. She left a message saying the owner of the property in Westchester Heights Community has accepted my offer and she would be in the office until 8 o'clock pm. It was just was a little after 5 pm so I had enough time to drop Albert off at his place and make it to Ms. Janet Walker office by 6:30 pm. I flew the CC to the outer bounties of town and drove Albert to his place. I told Albert if I have time I will come to his Comedy Club "Crowning Around" later tonight. As I left Albert's place I called Ms. Walker to let her know I got her message and I was on my way to her office.

I arrived at Ms. Walker's office. She saw me pull up so she greeted me at the door. We walked back to her office. She had some paper work she needed me to fill out. The owner wanted to go to closing in the next couple of days. I was fine with that, for I was tired of living in the hotel room. After I filled out all the proper paper work we were ready to finalize the deal and by the weekend I would be moving in to my new home. I told Ms. Walker about my buddy Albert's new Comedy Club "Crowning Around", it was Brentwood new watering hole. And when she gets some free time she should stop by. Janet told me she haven't heard about it before but will check it out for she needs a good laugh now and then.

I arrived at Albert's club after meeting with Janet.

Crowning Around was an unique name I thought to myself. Crowning was in place of clowning, it was an eye catching name for a comedy club. The club hasn't yet been open to the public. Albert was still remodeling the building and getting the style of the room to where he liked it. He was booking comedy acts, hiring cooks, waitress, and bartender staff personnel. I went over there that night to see how things were going and to see if he needed any help with the remodeling.

Today I close on my new house; I'm planning to move in on Saturday. After the closing I am going to go furniture shopping, for a new house deserves new furniture. Arriving at the real estate office early to the get the process under way for I was excite to have the deed and keys in my hands. I wasn't much about borrowing money from a bank to buy a house for I wanted to own my house and not the bank owning it. I have seen many people lose the house they have made payments on for years because they missed a couple of payments after falling on hard times. I made a promise to myself that when I buy a home I would pay for it in cash. So this day is a great Thursday because I am paying cash for my dream home. The seller has arrived at the real estate office and the time has come for us to sign all the proper paper work.

Wow I had signed so many papers my hand had fell asleep. Now that I have the deed and keys in my hands I'm the proud owner of a new Westchester Heights Home. The closing took a few hours, but the excitement had me fueled so I went looking for furniture for the house. I stayed in the hotel two more nights for the furniture store wasn't able to deliver my new bed and other home furnishings until late Saturday morning, which gave me time to do some dusting and cleans without moving furniture around. The closing came at a great time, my professor job was beginning in the following two weeks. I didn't want to live out of the hotel room while I was teaching the class. Chasing down UFO's and keeping a job to stay undercover will prove to be challenge. The new chapter of my life has begun, and believe it or not it seen like a TV sitcom.

CHAPTER 5

NEW VARLDOION MAYBE

Time was of the essence to find a new suitable home planet. The survival of Ploutcraft's specie was crucially based upon Ploutcraft successfully completing his mission. With the weight of Varldoion on their shoulders Ploutcraft and Larker pushed their crew to the limits like never have before. After travel through the warm hole to Earth, Ploutcraft put together a search party that consisted of Larker, B'Elanna Linkasa and 17 Royal Guard members. He left the remaining 31 Varldoion Royal Guard members to operate the mother ship and to give them aerial support if needed.

Varldoion Sho'aunor'es scanned the Earth surface to get an idea of what life forms roam the planet. Ploutcraft needed to know if the Earth beings were of a higher specie than the Varldoionains. To search the planet he wanted to do so under a cloud of secrecy. He wanted to keep his intention of take over the planet from the earthling. To stay unknown they will have to pass as human being, which will take their mind control abilities. If the stronger specie were the humans then their mind control would not work and their cover would be blown once someone saw them.

Having their search party assembled they boarded the space drone to depart from the mother ship. B'Elanna Linkasa was at the helm, Ploutcraft 2nd officer, for she was the ship's navigator. After receiving Ploutcraft orders to leave the mother ship, B'Elanna Linkasa navigated the space drone across the night's sky and landed in the Texas desert. Earth atmosphere being similar to Varldoion's they were able to breathe the air. But Earth atmosphere just being slightly different than Varldoion gave the Varldoionains super abilities that they never had on Varldoion. They were not aware of the change of their abilities when they first step foot on the desert floor. Each Varldoionain received different super abilities from Earth atmosphere.

The search party began taking soil samples, atmosphere reading and monitoring the climate. They wanted to know what would be the long term effect for their specie to live on New Varldoion. So Ploutcraft run test to see what it would take to set up a colony on the planet. Though the desert was cool at night but the heat in the day wasn't something they were used too. So they wanted to search other parts of the planet to see if it was suitable for their specie. The Varldoionains had the technology to make the desert a nice paradise. They had alien tech which would shield the desert from the sun's heat during the day and store up that same heat and warm up the desert night. The Varldoionains could plant colonies all around the planet by adapting the earth's surface to them.

Ploutcraft wanted to observe earthling up close to see them interact with each other. They chose small western country towns to do their observations. They needed to know if the earthling would be a hindrance to their plans to inhabit the Earth. They walked among the humans to study their behaviors, the town folks never knew they were there. In their observation they learned humans were a people of war, for they were not one people. They disagreed and fought each other about many things. Ploutcraft wanted to use this to their advantage, for he knew a divide human race would not be able to stop them from subduing the Earth.

Months after arriving on the surface of the planet Ploutcraft began to notice the change that the atmosphere started to have on him. At first the change was gradually, it began with the ability to levitate which then developed into the ability of full flight. Each Varldoionain had similar experience with the new super abilities they developed by being on Earth. When Ploutcraft would take flight he would use his mind control ability to make the humans think he was a bird. Their present went undetected for several months, not even G.A.S knew they were on the planet when they first arrived. Ploutcraft and Larker started to study human behavior in Brentwood, Texas. Ploutcraft sent his Royal Guard two by two to study different parts of the planet.

G.A.S's spy satellites began to notice abnormal readings around western America. Ploutcraft and his Royal Guard would send their readings they collected back to their mother ship to complete a report for the Varldoionain Royal Council. G.A.S accidentally pick on these abnormal radar waves because their spy satellite would malfunction when Ploutcraft and his crew sent their data to the mother ship. The malfunction would cause the satellite to make field agent Albert Crown's communicator to beep uncontrollably. When his communicator started to beep repeatedly for no reason he took it to Tom Strathmore thinking it was malfunctioning. In Tom's investigation of the communicator he realized it wasn't malfunctioning but receiving a satellite frequency signal from an unknown source. Tom decided to keep Albert's communicator to run test to see where the frequency signal was coming from and what it was transmitting.

Tom's investigation uncover that the signal were originating from several parts of the planet several time a day going to space. One signal has been transmitting just outside Brentwood, Texas. He checked the spy satellite data, for it had intercepted all the data that Ploutcraft and his Royal Guard have transmitted to their mother ship. All the data was in an alien encoded form. Tom and James worked for months on end to see if they could crack the encryption but they were not having any luck. The code was in an alien Egyptian style hieroglyph alphabet.

The months spent trying to crack the code more data kept pouring in for the signals were still transmitting. One day drinking his coffee it hit James like a ton of bricks, he figured out how to crack the alien encryption. Ancient Egyptian hieroglyphs were similar to the alien hieroglyphs and if you remove the alien hieroglyphs that were different from the ancient Egyptian hieroglyphs he would be able to crack the code. Tom and James built a computer program that could read and remove the alien hieroglyphs that was different from the Egyptian ones. After completely cracking all the data they could translate it into English. Having the alien hieroglyph translated into English they were astonished by what the signal was transmitting.

"This is the report of Ploutcraft onto the Varldoionain Royal Council. Since the temperature of our world has dropped unto a degree we are no longer able to inhabit our planet because the life source has frozen over. You have sent my crew and I to search for a new planet for the 4 billion beings of our race to inhabit. Therefore we have found a planet called Earth in the Milky Way Galaxy. Earth is 200 light years from Varldoion. Its climate is continuously changing but with our technology I believe we can bring it under control. The atmosphere allows us to breath without any technology aide. The most amazing thing about Earth's atmosphere is that it gives each Varldoionain a different super ability that we didn't have on Varldoion. The human race that occupies this planet is a people of war, they are divided and I feel we being one people can conquer them by using our mind control to have them to do whatever we want. We can be the dominant race on Earth. As I continually to report back to you about our readings I feel we can make Earth into New Varldoion!"

Being totally shocked by what was happening right under their nose they needed a plan to stop an alien invasion from take over the Earth. Tom and James reported back to Director Beck their finding of the alien code. Learning that Ploutcraft race used brain waves to control lesser beings Nicole Beck ordered them to develop a device so they couldn't use their mind control on G.A.S agents. They put the G.A.S scientists to work to use their spy satellites to find Varldoion and do studies to see what was happening on that planet. For maybe they could stop them from invading Earth by seeing if they could help them fix what is wrong on their planet.

GETTING DOWN TO BUSINESS

The semester at Brentwood State University had officially begun, and we received the report of an alien outbreak around the country. It was now time for me to juggle my two lives. I had been priming myself for this for a while now. Getting down to business added new meaning to life, I needed to be the best multi-tasker I have ever been. Away from base I used my home and school office to stay on top alien activity that was happening. My G.A.S PDA was a handy tool I used to keep myself informed at school, I didn't want to use BSU computer equipment to log on to the G.A.S database fearing someone would track what I was doing and blow my G.A.S cover.

All agents were called into base to go through a briefing on what Tom and James discovered from our spy satellite. I had a good night sleep in my new home ready to start my day off searching for UFOs. Early that next morning I hopped in the SUV and drove over to Albert's place. I picked him up then headed over to base. Nicky greeted us as usual, with his smile and wave thinking we came to drop the SUV off to get some service done. So we smiled and waved back. Once down in the base parking lot we walked to the designated area where the briefing was being handled. I looked over at Albert and said *"it's time for the fun to get started"*. I was looking forward to this day since I was a child. If my little league teammates could see me now they would be totally jealous.

Director Beck welcomed everyone to the morning briefing. She started off by saying that there were coffee and donuts over on the side tables and we could help ourselves. I loved a tasty coffee and donut in the morning so my day was starting right. Getting my continental breakfast out of the way I could now focus on the meeting. She introduced Tom and James so they could start off the meeting with the report of their findings. Shocked by that there were aliens here in Brentwood right under our noses, and they have been here for months though we never knew it. If it wasn't for an accidentally beeping of Albert's communicator we still wouldn't have known it. When Tom informed us on the alien code translation my jaw down to the floor. I never in my wildest dreams thought we would be protecting the world from an alien invasion. This has taking my military experience to the next level.

I wasn't aware that someone or thing could use mind control over a person. Tom and James developed a new communicator with a Bluetooth device called SPMCB which stood for Smart Phone Mind Control Blocker. When you wore the Bluetooth in your ear it protected your mind by blocking the mind control waves. The thing was while you were sleep your mind would be vulnerable from attack by their mind control so they developed also a device called NCMCB which was short for Night Cap Mind Control Blocker. You wore this night cap while you were sleeping and you would be free from them controlling your thoughts at night. It worked in the same way as the Bluetooth worked.

Tom had done some research to find Varldoion with our satellites; they were able to locate it in the Jodajoton solar system. The planet was completely iced over. It was too far from its nearest star to receive heat. Deep in their planet's core it has developed its own heating source but it has ran out of energy to heat itself. James and Tom had come up with a plan to reheat their planet's core.

They constructed plans for the H=ET4 (Heat equals Energy Transfer through the Fourth Dimension). The plans were of satellite devices that would take the energy from their nearest star and transmit it through the fourth dimension and there would be a receiver at the planet's core that would receive the transmission from the fourth dimension to reheat the core. Over a matter of weeks the prototype H=ET4 would bring Varldoion out of its ice age. G.A.S gave me the mission to find Ploutcraft and deliver the H=ET4 plans to him to stop their invasion. So I was in charge of the safe keeping of the H=ET4 blueprints. After receiving the SPMCB, NCMCB and all the data and H=ET4 blueprints Albert and I went to start our search for Ploutcraft and his Varldoionain Royal Guard.

We left GAS 225 and went back to my home; I wanted to enter the data into my home computer. I know it would be more time efficient for us to work out of my house than out of our base office. The time saved from traveling to and from the base was very important. When we got to the house I lock the H=ET4 blueprint into my office safe which I had hidden behind a hologram wall that had picture of me striking a Heisman pose. I figure it would be smart to keep the blueprints in the safe until we were able to locate Ploutcraft.

Not knowing where to look for him, we enter the last known coordinates of the data that was taken near Brentwood. We had no idea of what to expect, we didn't know if he was friendly or hostile. Albert reminded me of the gun wheeling cowboys I have seen in movies. If there was a member in good standing with the NRA it was Albert. For he loved his guns especially the G.A.S issued high tech weapons. He would go often to the base rifle range to shoot them.

So I know if Ploutcraft wasn't friendly Albert wouldn't have a problem using his weapons to stop him in his tracks. G.A.S has issued all field agents with an electric pulse gun that use a large pulse of electricity to stop an opponent in its tracks. The Sleep Maker 2000 has enough power to immobilize a whole herd of elephants all at once on max power. Albert being the gun craze guy I knew him to be, he modified two Sleep Maker 2000 to fit what he thought the weapons should have been. Albert could make a weapon out of a few toothpicks and talcum powder if need be. The modification that Albert made to the guns was it shot a single ray of electricity and when making contact with the opponent it no longer formed a web of electricity around the opponent that immobilized them, he renamed them The Widow Makers.

It was getting late and I had my first class to teach first thing in the morning, so Albert and I agreed to call it a night. Albert hopped in his government issued Apollo MoonLight which was an alien tech vehicle that the Apollo missions found on the moon in 1969. It has been in a government surplus warehouse for years after they ran several tests on the vehicle. Albert saw it in the warehouse; he thought it was a stylist sports car he needed to have to fit his taste instead of a SUV. So he put a request in to Director Beck to get the car instead the usual issued SUV. The government approved Albert's request so they can have a better idea what the vehicle could do in the hands of a G.A.S field agent. Albert and I agreed to meet up after my class tomorrow to continue our search for Ploutcraft.

PLOUTCRAFT WHERE O WHERE ART THOU

The time has come for me to teach my first class Space Science 101 a beginner course to Aerospace. I went to my university office early to make sure I was fully prepared for class. As I got in my SUV and was backing out the driveway I saw one on my neighbors get in her car. She was a young woman so I wondered if she lived there with her parents for she looked no older than 20 and couldn't afford to live in this neighborhood by herself. So the morning drive was peaceful and the traffic to the university wasn't crowded. I made it to my office about 7 a.m. which was great it gave me an hour to get done what I need too.

Before I knew it, it was ten minutes to 8 and I need to make my way to the classroom to teach the course. As I stepped foot in the hallway, the floor had to been magnetized for my bottom jaw dropped. I saw an angel in all her glory is how I can best design it. Monica Hamilton the new professor of art walked passed my office door as I was walking out the office. I could have sworn I heard heaven's angels sing when she walked passed me. I had to get to know who she was. Never before had a woman grabbed my attention in this manner. She made me lose my focus for a moment for I forgot what I was doing and where I was going. Once I got my composure back I remembered I was heading to the classroom so I rushed across the street to the Miller Houston Science Building. My classroom was on the third floor so I jetted up the stairs and made it to the room with two minutes to spare.

I walked in to the room calm; I didn't want to seem nervous though I was a little bit. I had my mind on finding Plout-craft, getting to know Monica Hamilton, and teaching Space Science 101. My focus to say the least was torn between these three things. I looked over my lesson plan, started class with roll call, when I got to the name Cecilia Martinez it was my next door neighbor who I saw leaving home this morning as I was leaving for work. The first class was all about what the course would be about. 101 is the beginner course where we would discuss the sun, moon, star, and the planets in the Milky Way. If time permitted we would even discuss how the ancient world thought about these things. After passing out the course sylla-bus and what to except I discussed the first chapter in the text-book. I told the class to read chapter 1 and 2 as the homework assignment for we will be discussing it in our next class in a few day. I asked Cecilia if she could stay after class. I want to get to know who she was since she was my next door neighbor and was a student in my class.

"Hi Cecilia I am your next door neighbor Professor Josiah Lewis. I saw you this morning leaving home and I want to introduce myself. Do you stay there with your parent?"

"Hello Professor Lewis it is very nice to meet you. No I don't stay here with my parents; they passed away when I was young."

"Cecilia I am so very sorry to hear that. So you don't have any family here in Brentwood?"

"I have a Grandmother back in Peru, but no family here. When my parents died in a car accident I was 6 years old and went to live with my grandmother. After I turned 18 I decided to come to col-lege here but didn't want to stay on campus for I didn't like the living conditions. So I got a place in the neighbor."

"Wow Cecilia it appears that you have been through a lot in a short time. I am glad to have you as a neighbor and I hope my class will be fulfilling to you. If you need anything or have any questions don't be afraid to ask."

"Thank you Professor Lewis, I do look forward to taking this *class, for from a young age I long to learn about space."*

"You are very welcome Cecilia; I hope you have a good day. I will see you in our next class later this week."

I ran back across the street to my office to drop off my school supplies, and head out to meet Albert to continue our search for Ploutcraft. Albert started the search this morning just east of Brentwood. So I hopped in the Calvary-Cross and drove out of town heading east. I called Albert to see where exactly he was. We know one the satellites signals was just east of Brentwood. We didn't know where exactly, the signals came from several places around the country that were received at the same time. There were ten signals that the satellite intercepted at one time. This tells us that there more than one alien sending out these signals that happen simultaneously. So knowing this Ploutcraft may not be in the region where the Brentwood signals came from. It is a great possibility that Ploutcraft may be in another part the country.

I met Albert at the desert site where the data originated from. He had looked around for a bit before I got there. By my arrival he was sitting in his MoonLight trying to stay cool, the heat has risen up during midday on an early August day. He had seen some parcel footprints. He had scanned them into the PDA then uploaded them to the G.A.S database. The prints were not recognizable. We could not tell if it was a shoe print, animal print or what it was that made the prints.

Albert showed me the locations of the prints. So we took a soil sample the prints and the surrounding areas. I wanted to run a chemical analysis of the sand in the footprints and the sand of outer areas of the footprints. Albert outfitted a small lab in the trunk of his car. It came in handy when we needed to run samples in the field and didn't have to take them to the base. There were 20 parcel footprints. By the look of the prints the wind had blown part of the prints away. So we took 40 soil samples, 20 from inside the prints and 20 from outside the prints. We run the chemical analysis on all 40 samples. The footprints came up with high traces of Eos Asta (a rubber like material), which is an alien elements. When Eos Asta is combined with silver it has the property that's stronger than steel but is lighter than aluminum. This element is found throughout Albert's Apollo MoonLight.

From the results of the chemical analysis of the soil samples of the footprints; the prints were made by feet that had high traces of Eos Asta. We know Eos Asta isn't found on Earth, but it's an alien substance that the U.S. government discovered in Roswell, NM in the 1950's when a UFO crashed in the desert. It's our theory that the prints were left here by aliens wearing some type of feet wear. We send our findings and soil sample to Tom and James in the base lab by teleport mail.

The teleportation of solid objects from one point to another point was an invention of Thomas Edison. In 1866 Edison at the age of 19 became a telegraph operator in Louisville, Kentucky. He started wondering if it was possible to teleport solid objects from Point A to Point B. Thomas Edison developed a theory for teleport base on the telegraph. Telegraphs sent beep sounds along a wire from Point A to Point B. An operator at Point A would transmit the message with beeps; it would travel down the line to Point B where an operator would receive the beeps and there translate it back into word form. So he wondered if you could change a solid object into air waves and transmit it to another place and change the air waves back to the solid object. It wasn't until 1900 when Thomas Edison made his teleportation theory a reality. The U.S. Government took Edison's invention to use it in World War I. They kept it locked away so no one would know that Edison had invented teleportation. For this technology in the wrong hands would be dangerous. Thanks to Edison I don't have to travel back to base to send or receive my packages.

It was getting late and Albert's Grand Opening of his club was tonight and we needed to head back to town to get everything for the 8 o'clock opening. Albert said *"Josiah I will meet you at the club by 7 o'clock. I need to go home and change."* I said to him *"Okay Albert I will meet you there after I change also."* We expected a lot of people for the Grand Opening. Albert ran a TV ad on the local TV station WBTS. The ad was running for 3 weeks, so the whole town knew that The Crowning Around Comedy Club was the new place where it was happening. With not much night life to do in Brentwood the comedy club will be popping!

I drove straight home with the day's activities on my mind. This was my very first UFO field work and I didn't want to blow it. Too many lives were on the line and I could not afford to make the wrong decisions. We had no idea where we could find Ploutcraft. I felt like I was in an Old English play that would have been called *"Ploutcraft Where O Where Art Thou."* Though we knew that aliens were in Brentwood, we have no knowledge if it's Ploutcraft. I feel time is of the essence to find him before they develop a plan for invasion!

A NIGHT FULL OF LAUGHS

I arrived home with a little time to spare before I need to meet Albert at the club. I pull the SUV into the garage. Getting out of the SUV I walked through the garage door into the kitchen. I felt the need for a big glass of ice water. Being in the desert heat had made me very thirsty. After gulping down the ice water in record time I headed up the back stairs to my master bedroom. I walked to my walk-in closet to get my black tux and tie to lay them out on the bed. I also got my black patent leather tux shoes and sat them on the floor by the bed. I was in need of a long shower for I sweated out my clothes. The Texas summer heat caused me not to be my freshest. After a long hot cleansing shower I shaved my face and brushed my teeth. I got dressed in my tux and patent leather shoes and spayed myself with my best smelling cologne.

Heading out the garage I drove across town to the comedy club. Janet Walker greeted me at the front door. She took a part time gig at Albert's club as a hostess. The real estate market sales were down so she needed extra money. I introduced her to Albert, and after talking with her. I asked her if she like to be his hostess knowing that she was in need of a part time night job. Janet told me how real estate market sales were down in the last six months. I know Albert had a need for a hostess so I told him he needed to talk to Janet for she could use the money.

Albert was the MC for the grand opening. He booked a few comedy acts like funny man Stevie Paige, Terry Tate, and Mercedes Williams. Stevie had been running the local Texas comedy circuits. Both Terry and Mercedes were Brentwood locals that Albert was giving chances too to start their careers. Albert hired a couple of gourmet chefs to make his comedy club to have a five star restaurant atmosphere. Albert hasn't spared anything for the grand opening; the club was design to resemble the Harlem, NY Cotton Club of the 1930's. Everything from the curtains to the table cloths were of the style of the Cotton Club. The best Texas jazz band Scatz was hired to play at the club nightly. The club wasn't the type where you showed up wearing a pair of jean and a t-shirt. It was a formal dress to impress type of club that you would find in a big city like New York but Albert made its roots here in Brentwood, Texas where we do everything big.

I was wondering who would show up for Albert's opening night. I had my hope that Monica might maybe come. I wanted to get to know her, and tonight could be a great opportunity for that. The door opened at 8 o'clock p.m. and people started to flood in. Janet being the Hostess began to seat people; Crowning Around employed a five star waiter and waitress staff. People who didn't want a table could sit at the top of the line bar that Albert installed in the club.

To my amazement Monica Hamilton walked in wearing a gorgeous pink and purple gown, and she was alone. I asked Janet to seat her at my table since there were not many tables left for the club was standing room only by 8:30. I introduced myself to her.

"Hello I am Professor Josiah Lewis, but you can call me Josiah. I saw you this morning when I was leaving my office in the Alicia Fitzgerald Art Building. I am a new professor at BSU."

"Hi Josiah, it is very nice to meet you. My name is Monica Hamilton. I teach a class in the AFA building. I am an art professor at BSU. I have been here a years now. I am from Harlem, NY. I was an artist when I lived in NY. I took a job here to teach college students art for I need a life change."

As we began to talk Scatz was playing some of the lovely jazz music. Albert walked on stage to start the night's entertainment. Him being the MC I expected so good opening jokes.

"Ladies and Gentlemen I am Albert Crown, Welcome to Crowning Around we have a full night of entertainment in store for you tonight. Our house band Scatz will play some of the best jazz, pop and R&B music for you tonight. Feel free between acts to get up and dance. We have three of the finest young comedians here for your laughter enjoyment."

"You know there isn't nothing like a sexy woman but two or three sexy women.... hahaha...... And Ladies you all are looking sexy tonight and if your men don't think so my number is on the stalls in the ladies room.... But all jokes aside coming to the stage is a young man that thinks he is God's gift to women too bad he is the only one that thinks that..... hahaha.... Give a big hand of applause to Terry Tate or you may call him Tee Tee..................."

The night has started with a bang and hopefully all will go well for Albert's grand opening. Tomorrow we will restart the search for Ploutcraft but tonight the only thing on my mind was getting to know Monica. Terry had some good jokes. He made a lot of funny jokes that made Monica and I both laugh. Albert said after Terry's act there will be a thirty minute break before the next comedian so feel free to get up dance and enjoy the music.

I asked Monica if she would like to dance and she said yes. The dance floor that Albert had in the front of the club near the band was a very nice black shiny tile. Scatz began to play some good slow love music. Monica and I began to slow dance and she pulled me tight to her and I toned everything else out for all I saw and heard was her. Being 6'4" I was a foot taller than her, so dancing close she was looking up at me. I loved the fact I got to look into her pretty brown eyes.

She said to me *"You have the nicest hazel-green eyes, and I can't stop looking into them. I saw you this morning looking at me for I was looking at you too! You are a very handsome man. I came here tonight hoping you would be here."*

"I had no idea you saw me. I was stumbling and fumbling all over myself when you walked by, I never noticed if you saw me. I saw you walk to your office and I looked at the name on the door. I had your name in my head all day and couldn't wait to I got the opportunity to meet you. When I saw you walk in tonight I told Janet to seat you at my table."

"Oh I see..... I had you messed up this morning as you have me tonight.... I really like the way you look in this tux..... I can feel your heart beat dancing this close to you. I was wondering who you were for I never seen you before today. I didn't know your name for your office didn't have a name tag."

Yea... They are getting around to putting my name tag on my door. It should be up next week. They didn't have room for me in the science building so they gave me an office in the art building."

We danced romantically around the dance floor as the music gently blew us around and around as the wind blowing a leaf on a cool fall day. When the music stopped we walked back to our table. Albert came out and introduced the next comedian, Mercedes Williams. She had a funny jaw dropping act. I don't know way Albert found her at but he may have just discovered the next bright star. She was a raw talent who knew how to deliver a punch line. After her act we decided to dance some more.

Her presence was intoxicating, like a drug I needed more and more. These feelings I have never felt before. I was addicted at the first dose of her attentiveness to me. I have heard of love at first sight but I never believed it to be true until now. I was wrapped up as a Christmas gift the first time she said Hello! If Santa Claus was real I would have been a present under her tree ready to be unwrapped on Christmas Morning. As my charm had her caught up so did her grace and beauty had me captivated.

The night had seemed short but Albert had one more comedian act Stevie Paige. He was known as the Texas Funny Man and people would travel for miles to just see him perform.

He was Albert's main attraction for the evening. At his introduction there was a standing ovation for this what everyone was waiting on. Monica told me she was a big fan of his. Our dinner came just before he started his act. Normally his act lasted about an hour so if it was the same tonight it would give me a little more time to spend with Monica.

Monica and I had just finished our dinner half way through Stevie Paige act. During his act people were still wandering in. Albert just happened to be standing in the back by the bar when a couple waltzed in. I wasn't paying it any attention because Monica had all of it I could give. Albert having his mind control blocker Bluetooth in his ear noticed what no one else did. He saw from the corner of his eye two strange looking beings.

The male alien was tall and slender; he had a shiny milky white skin, and it had a long slender oval shape head with long straight navy blue hair. His nose was long and straight. He had a mouth that is medium in size with thin black lips. His teeth were sharp and pointy as shark teeth. He had a long slender neck. He also had two eyes that are a solid baby blue color. Strangely enough they walked upright on two legs. Their arms are long with human like hands. The male wears a two piece spacesuit that was twilight lavender and black with black space boots. The female alien was very similar to the male but she looks very feminine. Her skin texture was similar to his; she had long wavy style hair that was as red as fire which goes the entire way down her back. Her eyes were a solid bright emerald color. Her lips were the same color of her hair. She wore a female space dress that was Onyx and Jade in color with matching Onyx boots.

When I heard Albert yell "*You don't belong here!!*" I looked around and shocked by what I saw for I also was wearing my Bluetooth I ran to the back. I didn't know if one of the two aliens was Ploutcraft but I could assume one was. But sitting in the front of Albert's huge club I could not make it to the back as my crazed two gun wheeling partner pulled out his two modified G.A.S issued guns Widow Makers . As he shot both guns saying; *"It's time for you bums to go Beddy Bye!"* They had hair triggers, the female alien push the male alien out of the way to protect him. By doing so she took both blasts from his Widow Makers that Albert had set to full power. The blast made a double hole fhrough her and she dropped to the club floor like a sack of potatoes. The male seeing the female on the floor and not moving levitated and hopped out of the building quickly.

The whole comedy club was in an uproar. I quickly threw a table cloth over the alien body and put it behind the bar before any one saw the alien. Some people thought it was all a part of Stevie Paige act. Albert went to the stage to calm down the crowd. He said *"Exclude me Ladies and Gentlemen there was an attempted robbery so the authorities have been contacted and we need to evacuate the building calmly and quickly as possible."*

I escorted Monica outside safely while Albert waited for the G.A.S extraction team to arrive. I asked her did she have a ride home or did she need a cab. She told me she took a taxi to the club. So I called the nearest cab company to make sure she got home safe. I asked her was it possible for me to see her again and she said yes. We exchanged numbers and she told me to call her. I told her I would for I looked forward to talking to her again. The taxi cab showed up not shortly after I called them. I paid the driver so she would not have too. I said to the driver take her home and she told him her address.

Not long after she left the extraction team showed up disguised as Texas State Law Enforcement and EMTs. As they pulled around back of the club and taped off the perimeter the local news station WBTS channel 36 showed up on the scene. I stayed outside to do my best spin doctor. I called over to the reporter Dominik Prince, who was a Ukrainian exchange student that graduated with a journalism degree from BSU and had his first reporter job at WBTS, to throw him off the news trail. I said to him *"I am Professor Josiah Lewis from BSU and I saw what hap-*

pen for I was on my way to the men's room when it went down." So he took me to the side to do an interview.

His camera man set up the lighting to get the interview on TV so now I would see how good of a spin doctor I would be. The camera man said *"Interview take one in 5,4,3,2,1, go."*

"This is Dominik Prince of the Channel 36 news team and I am stand here with Professor Lewis of BSU. Can you tell what happen inside of Crowning Around?"

"Okay, half way through the Stevie Paige performance I decided to get up to use the men's room. As I started to walk to the back of the club from the front I saw two people enter the club doors and walk over to the bar. I heard one of them say this is a stick up give us all your money. And as the club owner pulled out his shotgun at the same time pushing the silent alarm I guess, one the robbers shot at him and missed. How he missed I don't know. Seeing the owner's shotgun after missing the shot the two robbers fled the club not wanting a Mexican standoff I would assume. The owner cleared the club and waited for law enforcement to show. They showed not long before you and your camera crew did."

While he was buying my spin on what happen a G.A.S extraction team member disguised as a Texas State Patrol Officer came to me and said *"Sir we need to talk to you inside to find out what you saw tonight."* So I said *"Yes Officer."* Dominik thanked me for my time and I responded to him and said *"Mr. Prince you are very welcome."*

I walked into the club to see how the extraction and cleaner up was going. I asked Albert was she alive and he told me he didn't know. All he knew was that she didn't seem to be moving. A double blasted at full power from the modified Widow Makers would kill most things. I guessed that her fate wasn't much different. We bagged her and laid her in the back of the EMT to transport to GAS 225 so Tom and James could examine her further. The spin we told started to work quickly for the eye witnesses and staff member were saying that's what they saw. It happen so fast they didn't know what they saw and once we said what they saw they started to believe that was what happen.

The reporters, crowd and extraction team were gone. I help Albert clean the club for he had sent his staff home early so they wouldn't stumble over any alien evidence. I told him don't worry about what happen it was an accident and we have it all under control. For my knowledge we did. And we will sort through it first thing tomorrow afternoon and submit our findings in a report to Director Beck in a few days. So after we finished cleaning and straightening up the club I told him to drive home and get a good night sleep for we had a few full days of work ahead of us. We locked up and walked over to our vehicles. He drove off as I started the SUV. I wondered to myself what would have happen if Albert didn't shot at the aliens. What if they would have hurt someone even yet have hurt Monica? I don't know what I would have done if something had happen to her. I am happy Albert's quick response save many lives tonight. I hope we find Ploutcraft before it's too late!

CHAPTER 6

LOSE LOVE OF ART

The year was 1915 George Thomas Dunaway of Richmond County, Virginia moved to Harlem, NY. George T. Dunaway would become one of the great music composers of the Harlem Renaissance in the 1920's and 30's. One cool fall night in 1923 George met a young beauty named Eugenia Foster at the Hollywood Club on 49th and Broadway. He would eventually fall head over heels for her. After a long three year courtship they were wed in holy matrimony. George was a musician from birth, it was a God given talent to hear the tones and rhythms of music.

This gift made George T Dunaway a great composer. These artistic talents were passed on to his offsprings. George and Eugenia had three children twin girls Elizabeth and Martha and a son Joseph Anthony Dunaway. Joseph would be known as J.A. Dunaway one of Harlem best poets of the 1950's. J.A. would have a daughter name Gloria Dunaway who was a song bird. Gloria had the voice of a nightingale. Gloria meets Charles Scott and falls deeply in love with him. Charles and Gloria Scott had one daughter Monica Scott.

Monica Scott inherited her artistic talents from her Great Grand Father George T Dunaway. Monica gifts were in the art of drawing and painting. By the age 18 Monica moved from Harlem to Manhattan NY. Only three years later she had 200 painting and drawings hanging on walls of galleries throughout Manhattan.

Monica's painting caught the eye of a young art gallery curator Robert E. Hamilton. Robert called Monica one day to discuss putting her artworks in many of his company art galleries around the country. They decided to meet in a small Manhattan coffee shop called Joe Man's Beans to discuss the business opportunity he was offering. They met in the coffee shop on an early Tuesday afternoon. As Monica's art captivated most people who saw it her physical appearance had that same effect on Robert.

After discussing the outline of his business proposal Monica lightly agreed until completed terms were nailed out. Enjoying each other's company they stayed at Joe Man's Beans for hours talking though their business discussions were done. Robert couldn't get enough of Monica for he didn't want the evening to end. But he knew this wouldn't last forever but only in his memory. Robert desired to get to know her better so he asked if she would have dinner with him the following night. Intrigued by Robert scenes of style Monica agreed to have dinner with him the following evening.

It was a love affair made in heaven, after dinner Robert and Monica took a nice stroll in Central Park. It was a beautiful evening, the moon light lit up the night sky. The stars were shining bright. It was a night that Doctor Cupid prescribed for two lost souls looking for love. It was like a dream come true for these two people to find each other. The more Robert got to know Monica the more he would grow to love her. Monica never thought she would find a man to love her unconditionally. Two and half years into the love affair, Robert would propose to her. With tears of joy Monica would say "YES". Robert Hamilton was the man of her dreams and now her dreams was becoming a reality.

Their engagement lasted for one and half years. The wedding was set for a bright mid Saturday afternoon in June. The chapel was packed with both their families and friends. Robert was standing at the alter with the pastor and his best man. The whole chapel was waiting on the entrance of one of the most beautiful bride even! Monica was escorted down the aisle by her father Charles Scott. The moment Robert saw her coming down the aisle tears began to run down his cheek. The day they waited on for four years was finally here.

   "Who gives the Bride away?" The Pastor asked when the Monica arrived to stand by Robert. Charles said *"I do."* Charles then took his seat beside his wife Gloria. The Pastor said *"Dearly Beloved we are gather here today to witness the union of this man Robert and woman Monica in Holy Matrimony."* Robert took Monica by her hand as Charles went to his seat. Monica's tears of joy began to steam down her face. She waited for the man to come in her life to love her like no one has before. Now Robert was this man, her joy was immeasurable. She loved Robert with her whole heart, he became her whole world. The Pastor asked Robert, *"Robert do you take Monica to be your Wife, to love her without conditions? Too honor her and respect her and give your all to her in sickness or health, for richer or poorer until death do you part?"* Robert responded by saying *"I Do!"*

   Then the Pastor said unto Monica, *"Monica do you take Robert as your Husband, to love him unconditionally? Too honor and respect him and give your all to him in sickness or health, for richer or poorer until death do you part?"* Monica answered, *"I Do!"* After the exchange of the rings the Pastor said *"Robert you may kiss your Bride!"* As Robert kissed Monica, all in attendants cheered with joy because two lovely souls had been united in love. *"I now present to you all for The First Time Mr. and Mrs. Robert Hamilton"*, the Pastor said. This day was one of the best days in Robert and Monica Hamilton life.

   Two and a half years later and three boys, life couldn't get any better for Monica and Robert. Like their wedding day starting a family was as glorious! Pregnancy was not easy for Monica but she was grateful that her Creator entrusted them with the lives of three little ones to bring up to be productive part of society. Robert was a hard worker but now that he had a family to care for he worked even harder to provide for them. He began to work harder to establish new art galleries to put

Monica artwork in. He started to travel more than he normally would.

A year after the birth of their twins Robert made a trip to Rochester in Upper State New York to open a new gallery. Robert told Monica that he would only be gone for a week. He needed to be there to help the Rochester's gallery with their opening. But three days after Robert left for his trip The New York State Police sent representatives to Monica home in Manhattan to deliver to her some tragic news.

The New York State Police Captain knocked on her door. She opened the door and said *"How can I help you?"* The police captain responded *"We are from the New York State Police. Are you Monica Hamilton?"* Monica answered *"Yes!"* Then she responded to Monica, *"May we come in?"* So Monica invited the two officers in. The captain said to her, *"You may want to take a seat. We were sent here today to deliver to you some tragic news!"* Handing Monica a formal letter, she continue to say to her, *"We are sad to inform you that your husband Robert Hamilton was killed in a terrible accident on North I-81 two days ago. He lost control of the car after running over a patch of black ice on a bridge on I-81. His car drove off the bridge and down the embankment. He was flown to the nearest hospital where he died just a few hours later from internal injuries."* As the captain was telling Monica of the death of her husband she began to scream uncontrollably, *"No, No, No, No!"* As her children heard her scream they began to cry, scared not knowing why their mother was screaming. The officers tried to calm her they asked her did she have anyone she could call to be with her in her time of need. She called her parents and told them of the tragic news. Shocked by the news Charles and Gloria traveled over to Monica's place as quick as possible. When they arrived at Monica's home the two officers greet them and explain what happen. After explaining it to Charles and Gloria what they told Monica the two officers left.

Gloria went to stop her grandchildren from crying while Charles tried to comfort his daughter. He knew not what to say so he held her as she cried uncontrollably. Her world just came crashing down for the love she waited her whole life for was gone without warning! She wondered why God would put her through this. Why He would take her husband from her and her children she asking while Charles tried to comfort her. Gloria and Charles didn't know what to say to her. Monica blamed her God given gift for killing her husband. She kept saying if I wasn't an artist Robert would still be alive. At that moment she began to despise her gift. No one would get any sleep for the next following days.

Robert's funeral was set a week after his death. The same pastor that performed their wedding was the one to oversee Robert's funeral. Robert's parents and family couldn't believe he was gone. The church was full of grief, Robert was truly loved but no one loved him more than Monica did. As the Pastor began Robert's ullage Monica was crying because her grief. The female ushers tried to comfort her to calm her. It worked for a little while but when the Pastor would say Robert's name again she would start crying thinking about life without him. After the funeral friends and family members would come up to Monica and Robert's parents telling them how sad and sorry they were of his passing. And if there was anything they could do they would be there for them!

Monica and her children moved in with her parents' home for a few months. She couldn't stay at her place for everything reminded her of Robert. Her grief being so great had her heart not able to take continuing being reminded he was gone! Despising being an artist she gave up painting. She sold her home in Manhattan and rented an apartment in Harlem near her parents. Robert's sales of her art in his company's gallery and his life insurance she was able to survive a few years without working.

It was now three and half years after the passing of Robert. Monica knowing it was time to move on; especially it was something she needed to do for her children well-being. She began looking for career opportunities outside the state of New York. All she knew was being an artist, but didn't want to paint again; she thought maybe she could teach art. She sent applications to different schools around the country that posted jobs for an art teacher.

One school who received her application was a lover of her art would jump at the opportunity of having one of the greatest artist of the 20th century to teach their students. She could really boost their art department. Brentwood State University sent Monica a job offer letter without ever interviewing her. They offered to provide her with housing to help her with the transition after receiving BSU offer. Monica discussed it with her parents. They thought it was a opportunity for her and their grandchildren though they would terribly miss them a lot. Charles and Gloria knew this was the opportunity that Monica needed to get on with her life after the passing of Robert. They felt leaving New York was what Monica needed to start her moving on. Agreeing with her parents, Monica contacted Brentwood State University to inform them that she was accepting their offer. She wanted to start teaching their following fall semester. It was now spring so she only had a few summer months to prepare her and her three sons for the move to Brentwood Texas.

Monica having her affairs in order flew to Brentwood for a week. It was the middle of the summer and she needed to meet with BSU board members to sign her acceptance letter. BSU had a nice program to help out of state faculty to find affordable housing. Monica met with the program leader to help her search for the most suitable housing for her and her children. She needed a home that had enough space for her and her three sons and that would not exceed her budget. Janet Walker who was the local real estate agent helps BSU with their faculty housing program. Janet contacted Monica to find out what her housing requirements would be. After talking to Monica, Janet searched her database to see if there were any houses for rent that matched what Monica was looking for.

Monica went to look at the houses that Janet found in her database that was for rent. She had an idea of a modest four bedroom two bath house in a nice neighborhood that she wanted. There were some that the interior was not good enough for what she was used too while others were a little too pricey in rent. It seemed like the Goldilock and the three bears, too hot, too cold and just right when Monica found the home that's just right for her. Janet helped her with the application process to lease the house. Before the end of her trip Monica had set up everything that was needed to start teaching and found a place for her family.

When Monica got back home to Harlem NY Charles and Gloria helped her pack all her stuff for the move to Texas. Monica wanted to settle down in their new home a few weeks early before she had to start teaching her art classes. Charles packed all her stuff in the truck he rented to drive to Bentwood TX. Charles and Gloria drove the rental truck while Monica and her three sons followed them in their family car. After her parents helped her settle into her new home Charles returned the truck to the rental office.

It was a sad goodbye though Charles and Gloria knew this is what she needed to start her life over since the tragedy. For it would be a little while before they would see her and their grandsons next summer. Monica drove her parents to the local airport so they could catch a flight back to Harlem. With tears in everyone eyes Charles and Gloria boarded their flight while Monica and the boys waved goodbye. Monica drove the boys to the local fast food restaurant for a quick lunch before they head back to their home. A new era had begun for Monica and her sons in a new home in a town with a new job, who knows what the future may hold for them all!

MISSING YOU R.I.P

Treasure means a lot for many people then to others it means a lot more. Some love their treasure so much they would even take it to the grave with them though they have no use for it there just to stop others from having it. Then there are people that would stop at nothing to get the treasure not even the grave.

Cecilia Martinez is a young Peruvian girl from the city of Lima. Cecilia was from a loving home. Her parents worked hard to provide Cecilia with everything she needed in life. The Martinez was a couple that had an eye for business. They loved the local market place. They often would search for treasurable things to sale at the local market place in Lima, Peru. Alfredo Martinez met Rebeca Perez and knew at first sight she would be the one for him. A few years after Alfredo married Rebeca, Cecilia was born. Alfredo was a Class A Treasure Hunter and he introduced the art of artifact hunting to Rebeca. At first Rebeca didn't like the idea of hunting for artifacts but when the thrill of the adventure of the hunt got in her blood it became an addiction. Her pregnancy with Cecilia couldn't stop her from hunting for treasurable goods with Alfredo.

Alfredo opened up a trinket shop to sale pottery and beaded jewelry in the local Lima market place to set up a front for their black market items. High class clients came from all around the world to buy their highly sort after valuable artifacts. Alfredo had set up a circle of clients and if a person wasn't recommended by a client from the circle they would deny the knowledge of any black market items. Alfredo and Rebeca knew that any law enforcement agent could claim to be a black market client. Selling black market artifacts to uncover law enforcement agents would jeopardize their nest egg that they had worked so hard to set up.

Many didn't know the legend of the origin of the Inca's artifacts like Alfredo Martinez. There was a spoken legend of the Incas that was told to the public, but a secret underground Peruvian sociality told of a different origin. They called themselves Hijo Del Dios which was Spanish for Son of the God. Alfredo was a member of Hijo Del Dios. Hijo Del Dios spoke of an Inca origin that was out of this world. The legend told of eight alien exiles who were banished from their home planet for criminal acts against their species. The eight alien exiles wandered the universe until making their way to earth. They found themselves what is today's Peru. Their spacecraft bore a hole in the mountain when it landed on Earth. Their leader Eyer-Mensa told the other seven exiles this would be their new home.

The eight exiles were four males and four females; the males were Eyer-Mensa, Eyer-Sesha, Eyer-Eose, and Eyer-Osho. The female exiles were Nomo-Uskka, Nomo-Vera, Nomo-Jioso, and Nomo-Supo. Eyer-Mensa leaded the exiles out the cave that their ship bore to conquer the natives that dwelt in that land. The people that they conquer served the exiles. The exiles mated with the conquer natives and the race of the Incas were born. The exiles taught the new race of people their traditions and gave them their sacred artifacts to protect.

Alfredo Martinez beginning a member of Hijo Del Dios and a follower of the legend knew of the areas to search for these artifacts. Many Incas took the artifacts to their graves just to protect them. But the grave couldn't protect the artifacts from artifact hunters like Alfredo. The Peruvian law enforcement didn't know of the origin of the Incas artifacts but had a speculation of Alfredo and Rebeca Martinez illegal dealing of the Incas sacred treasures. The Peruvian government started an investigation to tail the Martinez to gain evidence of their illegal dealings.

The Martinez learning that the Peruvian government was hot on their trail, so they took out a life insurance policy and set up a trust fund from their nest egg for Cecilia just in case something happen to them. While the Martinez were treasure hunting some would call it grave rubbing, Cecilia spent a lot of time with her grandmother Mary Perez which was Rebeca mom. Mary didn't know much about what her daughter Rebeca and son in law Alfredo were doing other then they ran a profitable trinket shop in the local market place. Mary loved the fact that she got to spend lots of time with her granddaughter Cecilia.

Rebeca and Alfredo took some time off from their artifact searching to spend time with Cecilia for they knew in a few weeks they would be so busy they would not have time to do so. It was a great two weeks that they spent with her. Cecilia beginning just six years old loved her parents so much. Being at her grandma's was fun but there were nothing like being in mommy and daddy's arms to her. After a relaxing and peaceful two weeks with Cecilia they had plans to travel from Lima to Machu Picchu to search for an artifact called the dagger of invisibility. For whoever holds this dagger would be invisible to their enemies.

The PNP was in hot pursued of the Martinez couple looking to catch them red handed with an artifact. Alfredo seeing the PNP was tailing them in the distance tried to elude them. Noticing that Alfredo speeded up to evade them the Peruvian National Police began to chase. Alfredo started to weave in and out of traffic to escape the presence of the PNP. Having a couple of artifacts in the car with them Rebeca knew if the PNP caught them with the artifacts they would be arrested. Fear gripped her thinking that all they work for would be gone pulled out her hand gun began to shoot at the PNP while Alfredo weaved in and out of traffic. Being shot at the PNP fired back to end the pursuit.

As Alfredo turn the wheel to get around a vehicle in traffic a PNP bullet struck his front tire. He lost control of the vehicle because of the blown tire their vehicle struck the car they was trying to get around. Their vehicle flipped in the air and when it came down another car hit them. The accident caused their vehicle to begin leaking gas and the heat of the vehicle's engine ignited the leaking gasoline and there was a huge explosion. Alfredo and Rebeca Martinez perished in the multiple vehicle explosion.

The explosion destroyed the artifacts that the Martinez was transporting so the PNP lost any evidence of the Martinez illegal artifact dealing. With the deaths of the Martinez the PNP had to close the case of any illegal actives that they may have been doing because they had no evidence to prove otherwise. Their will stated upon their death that two thirds of their funds and along with two thirds of their life insurance would go in a trust fund for Cecilia which she would have access of when she turn eighteen years of age. The other one third of their funds and life insurance policy would go to Mary Perez to pay for their funeral and to take care of Cecilia until she became of age.

Mary never let Cecilia forget who her parents were the older she became. Alfredo kept a journal of his life up to the day Rebeca and him pass away. He willed on Cecilia eighteenth birthday that she will receive the journal so she could know all about Rebeca and his life and business. Life with her grandmother was different than it was with parents. It took weeks for Cecilia to realize her parents was never coming back home when she was six years old. Though Cecilia loved her grandmother Mary she began to really miss her parents.

The loss of Alfredo and Rebeca Martinez left a void in her heart that no one could fill. Mary did all she could to comfort Cecilia but the older she became the larger the void in her heart grew. Cecilia felt the need to connect with her parents after their death but didn't know how to do so. It wasn't until her eighteenth birthday when she received Alfredo Martinez's life journal that she realize how she would be able have a connection with her parents. Just months after receiving the journal

Cecilia made a decision to study aboard at Brentwood State University. Mary didn't know why Cecilia decided to leave Peru and study aboard. Mary being a supported grandmother supported Cecilia in her decision.

What Mary didn't know was the search of acknowledge about her parents drove her aboard to study at BSU. BSU had a great history program which she felt the need to know more about Peruvian history because of her father's journal. After she was accepted in BSU as a freshman exchange student Cecilia made her plans to move to Brentwood Texas. Mary came to Brentwood TX for a few weeks to help Cecilia get settle in for school. Just before classes were to begin Mary flow back home to Peru seeing that Cecilia was all settled in and really to state the new chapter of her life. Now being a young woman life for Cecilia would always be an adventure she wanted to explore.

CHAPTER 7

TAGGED AND BAGGED

Arriving home late I knew tomorrow would be a busy day. Albert and I would have to be at the base early to go over the details of tonight incident. We have in our possession a body of an alien life form. I know when Tom and James received the news they would be eager to run their test on the female alien. I had like a million thoughts running through my mind that made it hard for me to sleep. My mind raced all night long, thoughts of Monica, how do we find Ploutcraft and stop an invasion.

So when I did finally fall to sleep I had a strange life like dream. I was in a glass dome world with people I knew. It looked like Earth but some things were different then they are today. I guess it could be a vision of our near future. The night sky had a purple haze to it; we were not able to live outside the giant glass dome for the atmosphere was poisonous. We could not breathe outside the glass dome without breathing aide. The Earth we knew had change for the worst.

I was in a city with Monica walking on a nightly stroll; many people filled the streets this one night. As we walked I saw out of the corner of my eye a creature flying around outside the glass dome. It was not human, and it had no wings which cause it to fly. I said to Monica *"Look there is something flying outside the glass"*, and she responded to me by saying *"What is that? Is it one of the aliens that took over our planet?"* I said *"I believe it is, for it kind of look like the alien Ploutcraft."* As we were speaking it flew through the glass dome as if it had a window though it didn't.

It grabbed a person who was standing on the street corner and flew his outside the dome and dropped his on the ground. He began to gag for air; death was instantaneously having no oxygen in the atmosphere. The creature did this several times, and all I could do was watch in horror. Too our surprise it came after me and grabbed me by my ankles and Monica yelled for she feared I was about to die. When it grabbed me I kicked it with my free leg and it let go. But it wouldn't give up that easily. It flew around the dome to try for a second time to grab me to end my life. It flew through the glass one more time and as it came close to grab me I caught it in the air and body slammed it like if I was a pro wrestler. Being caught off guard it flew away not to come back again and at that moment I woke up.

This dream seemed so real to me, that it could have been a vision of what the world could be if we don't do something to keep the alien invasion from happening. The last thing I wanted to see was the lives of many innocent people being subject to alien rule. It was early morning and I had a few more hours before I needed to get up so I tried to go back to sleep. Being restless I just laid there unable to get my mind off of what we need to do. Before I knew it I fell back to sleep and my alarm clock went off and woke me up. So I got up and got myself together to start my long day.

I was out the door to go pick up Albert to head to the base to start our report. I arrived at Albert's place a few minutes early and he was still sleep. I knocked on his door but there was no answer for he was sound asleep. I don't know how he could sleep through this night for I knew I couldn't. I called him on my cell phone and he woke up.

"Hey Al are you still sleep?"

"Sorry Cap I forgot to set my alarm last night, just give me a few minutes and I be ready to go."

"No problem Al, take your time come out when you are ready."

Once Albert was ready we went to base, as we flew to base the sun rise was beautiful. I couldn't imagine myself not see a beautiful sun rise like what was in the dream. After we landed on the air stripe we drove to the base. Director Beck was waiting for us in our office to get the details of last night.

"Good Morning Gentlemen. How are you two today? I am glad y'all could make it in this morning."

I said *"Good Morning Ms. Beck. It has been a strange couple of days. But we are well."*

Albert responded also *"Yeah the last few days has been a little strange especially last night."*

"So gentlemen explain to me what went down last night?"

Albert began tell what happen. *"The night began as normal as it could have. I was the MC of the night event. I made a few funny jokes. The club was standing room only by the main act. Stevie Paige was half way through his act. And out no way the two creature came in the building. I guess they thought no one would notice them for who they really were so they came in to spy us out. But because of Tom and James device I noticed at once who they were. I reacted and yelled that they didn't belong here and pulled out my widow makers to shoot at the male creature but he moved out of the way. I shot the female creature instead."*

After Albert gave his point of view I chimed in and said, *"When I heard Albert yell I looked back and saw the two aliens. Before I could get to the back Albert had fired a shot. Striking and killing the female alien, we acted quickly evacuate the building and called for the extraction team to remove the body. There was a local news reporter outside the club I gave him a spin about a robbery and he bought it hook, line and sinker. The extraction team took the body to the base, Albert and I cleaned the club to make sure there was no evidence of alien presence left behind."*

She said *"Great job acting quickly! Wished Albert didn't go gun ho but nothing we can do about that now. Albert next time don't act so fast; take a little time to think. I believe you will have a next time. Now that they know we know they are here we will see them again."*

"Director Beck I will do my best not to be so gun ho, but I can't

promise in the heat of the moment I won't shot first and ask question second. Sometimes the excitement causes me just to come out with both guns blazing."

"I will try to manage the situation better, and help Albert not to shot first."

"Okay gentlemen I just hope you will handle the situation a little better next time. I will like your report on my desk by the end of the day. But before you finish your report make sure to visit Tom and James to get a run over of the alien body."

After talking to Ms. Beck, Albert and I started working on our report. Before our report could be finish we need to go talk to Tom and James to get the information about the alien body. We went down to level 5 where the science labs were. Tom and James offices were in the back half of level 5. After getting off the level 5 elevator we took the office rail car to Tom's lab. Tom's lab was a long walk from the front elevators so to save time it would be quicker to take one the mini inter office track cars, it was a six seat cart on a mini subway track. We arrived at their lab just in minutes to find James and Tom hard at work.

They got to work early this morning when they heard that they had an alien body to study. The excitement in the lab was like a kid on Christmas morning seeing Santa leaving him lots of toys under the Christmas tree. At this moment no one could play the role of Santa Claus better than Albert could for Tom and James. It was the first time in 50 years that American scientist had an alien to study. Quickly Albert became the scientists' superhero for his once in a lifetime delivery. So the moment we walked into Tom's lab all you could hear were applauses for Albert.

The approval of the scientists picked Albert's spirit up from our earlier meeting with Director Beck, which made him feel like he made a major mistake. Now feeling like a big man on campus Albert walked with his head hanging high. Tom and James greeted us with a hand shake. We were like rock stars in the science lab it was a wonder no one asked us for our autograph.

"Good Morning gentlemen," I said to Tom and James as we entered the lab. *"How are you two this morning? Hope y'all were able to get a good night sleep! I know myself I didn't sleep all that well, had a strange dream.*

James answered *"We are doing well here, as far as sleep goes, there were no sleep going on last night. The moment we received the word from the extraction team we all race back to the lab. No need to let our stiff get cold. Oh exclude my pun,"* James said.

We all laughed at his little joke. Albert said *"It was already cold; I put it on ice at the bar. It asked for a stiff drink and I gave it a drink on the rocks, ha ha ha."* He had the room in stitches as only he could. *"I guess it couldn't hold its' liquor,"* Albert said with a smile. *"I never seen such a pretty stiff but you know what they say, everything looks pretty when liquor is involved! But all jokes aside I hope we can learn about its specie from the study its body."*

I said *"Yeah that why we are here this morning to see if you have learned anything so we can add it to our report for Director Beck."* Tom answered *"We just began our study it may be a week or so before we can have the preliminary results. I will give you the basic body weight and measurements after lunch so you can add that to your report."* I thanked Tom and James for their help. We head back to our office to finish our report.

After getting the information we needed from Tom, we finish the report and placed it in Director Beck inter office mail box. With that out of the way we need to focus on the remaining aliens. Base off the alien DNA that was in the science lab Tom and James developed a tracking device. It homed in on their body chemistry up to a 100 miles radius. The DNA tracker would work on any species DNA that was input into the device. The device has 99.6 percent effectiveness. We got lucky when we were able to bag and tag the female alien to help us track down its companies. James called the DNA tracker the Blood Hound 50/50. Tom said he called it that because it was able sniff a person 50 times better than a blood hound and no one could out run the nose of a blood hound.

It would take Tom 12 hours to complete the programming the Blood Hound 50/50 to locate the aliens. I have a class in the morning so waiting on the tracker to be ready to proceed with our search will give me the time I need to work on my lesson plan. I hope I have some spare time tonight after completing my class work for tomorrow to call Monica. Having a full plate I am glad I know to do more than one thing at a time. My life has always been a jack of all trades and a master of all.

Our work day has come to an end; James gave us the Blood Hound 50/50 and told us it will be ready to operate in the late morning. So Albert and I left the base, I drop his at his place. He decided to reopen the comedy club tonight. I told him I would not be able to make it tonight for I had a little too much class work to do. It did seem like tonight would be a fun night but I was kind of sad I had to miss it. After I left Albert's place I went to the local Chinese restaurant Lu Wong Buffet to get carryout dinner so I could settle in for the night.

Now arriving home I settled down in front of the TV to eat dinner before I worked on my lesson plan. The local news was on TV, WBTS Channel 36 reporter Dominik Prince was on the tube reporting about last night club robbery attempt. They played a clip of my interview that I did with Dominik last night. Seeing myself on the nightly news was a little strange. Being in a small town now everyone knew my name and face. I would have to be extra careful not to blow my cover.

I started working on my lesson plan for tomorrow, it was a simple lesson that I wanted to go over. I want to do a lecture about the planets and stars in the Milky Way. Before it got too late I wanted to call Monica to just say hello and see how she was doing after what happen at the club. But before I could do that I had to complete my lecture outline and finish about an hour worth of lecture notes. What they say is true work always goes before play. I was totally looking forward to some good conversation with someone other than my G.A.S mates. Having a few minutes to get my mind off of aliens would help me keep my sanity.

Finishing my lecture notes I decided to give Monica a call. I had to go through my papers to find the number she gave me the night before. I dialed the number and it rang four times before she picked up. *"Hello, may I speak to Monica? This is Josiah."*

"This is she. Hi Josiah, it is very nice to hear from you. How has your day been?"

"It has been good, just been going over some work for tomorrow. I assume you got home save last night from the club?"

"Yes I did! Thank you for all you help seeing that I got here save. So did everything at the club go okay?

"Yea after the police left I helped Albert, who is the club owner and a good friend of mine, straighten up the place. It was late so he let his staff go home."

"That was really nice of you. I see that you are a very sweet guy!"

"Yeah I try to help my friends out whenever I can. And by the way I am sweeter than sugar cane! Ha ha ha! So be careful for you just might get a sugar high! Ha ha ha!"

"I believe I can handle it Sir! Ha ha ha. For I love lots of sugar in my sweet tea! The sweeter is for the better! Ha ha ha!"

"Monica, BSU is having their first home football game Saturday night would you like to go to the game with me?"

"I would love too, but I have no one to watch my three sons."

"No problem, bring them along with you we will make a fun time of it. I bet the boys will have a great time at the game. How old are your boys?"

"You sure it won't be a problem? They are 11, 10, 8 years old."

"No not at all! I have a connection in the university ticket office, for I am able to get unlimited number of discount tickets. So it's not an issue at all."

"Okay we will look forward to Saturday night."

"Monica it is getting late and I don't want to keep you up too late. Is it

okay for me to call you tomorrow evening?"

'Sweetie that will be fine! You have a great night sleep and sweet dreams."

"Okay my dear same to you and until tomorrow stay sweet!"

After our long phone talk I was a little sleepy. Note to self I need to have Awesome Blossum to enroll in Monica art class that she will be able to keep an eye on her for me. I wanted to write this in my task book so I won't forget that tomorrow. I have a long day tomorrow and I will need a good night sleep to get my rest so I can be able to face the day. Hopefully tonight it won't be a night of strange dreams. A dream like I had last night had me tossing and turning all night long, so I really didn't get much rest. But I believe this night will be different. It is lights out and time to hit the sheets. The stress of the world will have to wait a few hours while I sleep.

WHAT SHALL HE DO
WITHOUT LARKER!

This is the first time Ploutcraft has been apart from Larker since they been together as a couple. He was a little lost without her. He contacted B'Elanna Linkasa for he wanted to gather all of the landing party together and return to the mother ship to regroup. B'Elanna Linkasa piloted the space drone to retrieve all the landing party members from the spots they were sent to research.

After having retrieved all the members B'Elanna Linkasa flew to Ploutcraft location. Ploutcraft filled everyone in on the situation at hand. *"Larker has been killed by the humans! We walked into their place of gathering to spy them out. I don't know how they knew we were there. One of the humans pulled out a strange looking weapon he fired at us. She pushed me out of the way and he shot Larker. In my horror I saw the one I loved so dearly laying there dead! After their brutal attack I fled."*

B'Elanna Linkasa said *"How did they know Larker and you were there?"* Ploutcraft responded to her, *"This I don't know! I don't understand why our mind control didn't work on that human. No one else recognize our presence in that place but him. But we shall make them pay what they did to my love!"* Ploutcraft and his crew return back to their mother ship to gather their weapons and plan an attack for the loss of Larker. The G.A.S agents began their search for Ploutcraft not knowing that he and his crew left the planet to plan an attack.

Meanwhile back on Earth Josiah Lewis is about to start his day without any knowledge of what is about to go down.

What will this day have in store for us today? I thought to myself as I woke up to a new day. After I showered and got myself together I headed out the door to my office on campus to get ready to teach my class lecture. Tom has finished the programming of the Blood Hound 50/50 so after my class I will join Albert on the search of Ploutcraft. I am a little worry what will happen if we do not find him in time to hold off an invasion. But first things first I most get this class out of the way. I can breathe easier once I finish my lecture. I can do what I really get paid to do, protecting the world from space creatures is number one on my to do list.

Arriving at my campus office I picked up the phone to call Awesome Blossum. I wanted to inform her to pick up an art class as part of her cover identity. I had to make sure the line was secure before I called her. I ran a trace on the phone line with my G.A.S issued phone line device. I wanted to make sure that there were no listening or recording devices connected to the line. To be extra careful I hooked up my G.A.S phone call scrambling device. It was design to scramble the call info so if someone was trying to trace the call they would receive two fake phone numbers to protect the caller and the person receiving the call identities. And if the call was being recorded the recorded message would not be understandable.

"Hello Awesome. This is Josiah."

"Hi Agent Lewis. How can I help you?"

"I have a cover identity assignment for you."

"Do tell, I am in need of a good cover story."

"Since you are enrolled at BSU, I need you to take an art class taught by Monica Hamilton. I need you keep an eye on her to make sure

nothing happens to her. I want you to be my spy in her class to make sure no aliens enter her classroom."

"Agent Lewis I am happy to assist you with this. Thank you for trusting me with this assignment. I will enroll at once in her class."

"Okay, thank you for your help with this. If you have any issues contact me via my G.A.S communicator."

"Yes Sir I will. You have a great day!"

"Thank you and you do the same Agent Blossum!"

Now that I had set up protection for Monica I was less worried that something could happen to her. Awesome Blossum was a good artist who would be able to keep up in her class and do her agency duties. I had my lecture notes already printed off for my class so I left my office to walk across the street to the building where my class was held. I was a few minutes early, some of my students were just arriving for class. I pulled Cecilia Martinez aside and asked her if she would like to be my teacher's assistant and in return I would give her extra credit toward the course. She agreed to do so. When the class started she did the roll call. After she took the attendance I started the lecture.

"Good Morning class, today's lesson will come from chapter 1, 2, and 3. What is the Milky Way Galaxy? Planet Earth, our home, is contained in the Milky Way Galaxy. This name derives from its appearance as a dim "milky" glowing band arching across the night sky, in which the naked eye cannot distinguish individual stars. Milky Way is a translation of the Classical Latin from the Hellenistic Greek." One of my students asked me, *"Professor Lewis, is it true that the Milky Way Galaxy has at least 100 billion stars?"* I answered, *"Yes, it may contain up to 400 billion stars. The Milky Way began as small over densities in the mass distribution in the Universe shortly after the Big Bang. Some of these were the seeds of globular clusters in which the oldest remaining stars in what are now the Milky Way."*

After giving my first lecture I passed out the homework assignment for the next class. *"The assignment for the next class is to read chapter 3 and 4, I want you to start working on your 500 words essay papers on the making of the Milky Way Galaxy due in 2 weeks."* Dismissing the class I walked back to my campus office to finish up on some college work for the day. With my work completed I headed out my office door to walk to my SUV. It was time to find the Varldoionains. I called up Albert on my communicator to find out where he was so I could meet up with him. He told me he was at the club finishing up some things waiting for me to finish my lecture. So I drove over to the comedy club to pick up Albert so we could continue our search.

It was a hot Texas mid-day when I arrived at Crowning Around which was about high noon. Albert was in the back of the club getting things ready for the evening comedy show. Janet had some free time so she decided to help Albert to make some extra money. I knock on the front door of the club, Janet saw it was me and open the door for me. She said Albert was back stage so I went back there to see if he was ready to continue our search.

"Albert, how are things coming together in the club?"

He answered, *"They are coming together good. There were few new things we had to install in the club for tonight's show. We added new stage lights and a fog machine. This new act needed the fog machine for her act."*

"Oh wow really? That's a show I don't I want to miss. So let me know when you are ready to hit the streets."

"Ok give me a few minutes and I will be ready get down to business."

So I went outside to sit in the Calvary-Cross to wait on Albert to come out. I plugged the Blood Hound 50/50 into the Calvary-Cross GPS system. Since this was my first time using the device I wasn't too sure I was operating it correctly. Just when it came on Albert open the front passenger's door and sat in the seat. Tom has programmed it to pick up the Varldoionains' DNA. The scan began it search and picked up hits all around the state of Texas. We drove to the nearest point that the GPS had close to our current location.

Our anxiety was high for we didn't know what we would find when we arrived at the location that the GPS took us. Our task was of national security and the pressure was on us to be successful in our mission. I didn't want to be the one that cause our planet to be taking over by alien beings! We traveled 35 miles northeast of Brentwood. When getting to the place where the Blood Hound 50/50 brought us too there were no visual evident of an alien presence. Tom equipped the Calvary-Cross with a surface scanner. We scan the desert to see what we could pick up. That area was full of traces of Varldoionain DNA and high contents of Eos Asta (an alien rubber like material). The alien that was at GAS 225, its space dress and boots were made from Eos Asta.

We assumed that the desert heat cause the Varldoionains to leave high trace of their DNA there. The desert sand was like sand paper to their Eos Asta material they wore. As they walked around the desert floor the sand began wearing off the Eos Asta from their footwear. We drove to the next site that the Blood Hound 50/50 took us. We found the same things that we did at the first site. Site after site that the Blood Hound 50/50 took us too we found the same things. We needed Tom to fine tune the device because as it was it was leading us on wild goose chases. So we flew back to base to have the scientists to calibrate the device.

Nicky Jones waved at us like he did always with the thought of seeing us for the very first time as we drove up to the gas station entrance. Before we approach the base I called James to let them know that our arrival would be soon. The time was of the essence so we needed everyone ready to complete the task at hand in a timely matter. Albert and I hurried over to the science lab to meet James so that Blood Hound 50/50 could be calibrated as quickly as possible. When we walked in to the lab I wondered where Tom was for I didn't see him. James greeted us when Albert and I walked into the lab.

"Hey fellows, How have y'all evening been?"

I answered *"Hey James, been okay but it will get better when we get this tracker fix!"*

"Sure, I will see what we can do about that." James said. He took the Blood Hound 50/50 and gave it to the lab scientists to work on it. *"It shall take about 30 minutes for the calibrated. You can go grab a cup of coffee and a donut in the base café if you like then come back to get it when we are finish."*

Albert said, *"A cup of Joe would be great. Josiah, James has a good idea, let us go relax for a minute while we wait. It's been a long day, there is nothing we can do in here but get in their way. They don't pay me to work in here! Ha ha ha"*

"Yeah Albert, you're right, they have us doing enough as it is so no need for us doing their jobs too!"

James said, *"You guys are too funny, not! Ha ha ha"*

So we took the base shuttle to the café. It was a nice place for a government cafeteria. I haven't eaten since breakfast so I was a little hungry. So we decided to take a quick dinner break since we were in the café. We grab a cheeseburger combo meal with French fries and a drink. When we had finish eating it was time to go get the tracker. We took the shuttle back to the lab.

James said, *"Y'all didn't bring me a cup of Joe and a donut?"*

"I knew you were going to say that! Ha Ha Ha, That's why I told Albert we should bring you a Joe and a nut… hee hee hee"

Albert said, *"Yea James here is your bedtime snack. We all know you sleep here we seen your cart in the back. Ha ha ha! Nicole needs to charge you rent! Ha ha ha"*

James answered, *"If you two are finished with the jokes we have fixed the tracker. Plus I need to go in the back to get some sleep for its getting late! Ha ha ha"*

Albert said, *"Thank you James, now we will leave and let you go get your well needed Beauty Sleep!"*

James said with a smile, *"Like I said before y'all are too funny, not! When you need something else we will be here. So just let us know what we can do to help."*

I said, *"All jokes aside, Thank you James for all your help. When you see Tom tell him we said hey."*

"Sure I will do that. He is in one of the labs running tests on the alien y'all brought in. He had been busy with that since that night. I don't think he sleeps or eat. He been all about research, you would think he's a kid in a candy store." James answered with a sideways smile on his face.

We left the lab and went to our office before we left the base to pick up some needed supplies. We been at the base about an hour but it felt like an eternity with the world's safety on the line. Albert looked at me with this look on his face which was saying it's time for us to go. For we had been there too long! He locked our office door behind us and we walked to the SUV in the base underground parking lot. We got in the SUV and I plugged the Blood Hound 50/50 into the SUV scanner. We drove out of the gas station garage while Nicky Jones looked on.

Having the Blood Hound 50/50 calibrated Albert and I had the hope of quickly finding the aliens before they decide to start an invasion. Albert had a look of how much longer will this day be on his face. I called Agent Awesome Blossum while we were at base to get her to make some well needed sketches of the aliens. I thought maybe she could give us some possible looks of the Varldoionain specie. Albert gave Agent Blossum a description of the male alien that came into the club.

As we reached the runway of the base Agent Blossum e-mailed me a few of the quick sketches she drew based off of the alien that was at the GAS 225 and Albert's description. Albert and I download the data in to our PDAs. We had a sketch of an alien that could be Ploutcraft we assumed. Maybe the alien that fled Albert's club after Albert shot the female was Ploutcraft but we couldn't say with any certainty what it identity was.

Agent Blossum's sketch gave us a great visual of what the aliens look like.

Albert said to me, *"Hey is this thing working now."* He was referring to the Blood Hound 50/50. We turned it on and it wasn't giving us any readings. I responded to his, *"Yes it is working it was fine-tuned but it doesn't seem to be picking up any alien presence."* He looked at me with a funny look on his face and said, *"Don't tell me they fled the planet now that I am ready for round two."* I laughed because after our talk with Director Beck he was ready to throw down and fight. You would think fighting would have been the last thing on Albert's mind. We called James to let him know what was going on.

"Hey James, this is Agent Lewis. The tracker is not picking anything up. Albert and I have a feeling that Varldoionains have left the planet. Is there any way for the scientists to search Earth's orbit to see if there is a spacecraft orbiting Earth?"

James responded, *"I will get right on that. We did search when we got the signals from the satellite which we didn't find anything. Maybe they are there but we are not able to see them with our telescopes. I will get with Tom so we can develop a way to locate their spaceship."*

"Okay keep us informed. Meanwhile we keep the tracker searching and if it picks something up we have it send the data to our PDAs."

James said, *"That will work. We will inform Director Beck of the situation."*

Since we were not having any luck Albert and I decided to call it a day for it has been a long thirteen hours. I drove him to his place. He told me he was going to the club to help Janet oversee tonight's show. I want to get home so I could relax and call Monica. She crossed my mind since my search for Ploutcraft had come to an end for the day. I wasn't in to the comedy club scene tonight. I was looking forward to a deep conversation with Monica.

I got home shortly after dropping Albert off at his place.

After taking a hot shower and warming up a cold pizza I ordered a few nights before I decided to call Monica. She picked up the phone after the third ring. The sound of her voice to my ears were like a sweet red wine to a wine taster's palette. Her tone when she said *"Hello"* made my heart skip two beats. My stomach was filled with butterflies; it took a second for me to gather my composure. I said *"Hello Monica it is Josiah."*

"Oh hi Josiah you must just have scented me thinking of you. How are you doing today?"

"I am fine, just was doing a little work today. I guess it was because I was thinking about you too!"

"Oh I see! So what type of things were you thinking about?"

"Just the other night how I enjoyed spending time with you laughing and dancing the night away until the criminals came in trying to rob the club."

"I know right! That was so strange. Who would think in a million year that someone would come into a packed house that was standing room only and try to rob the place?"

"You are so right my dear. That was the strangest thing ever! You never know what's on a person's mind to make them think they could do something like that. I would think they would know better than to try anything like that in a crowd of people!" This I said to her thinking about the alien and not the story of two criminals coming into rub the club. She had no knowledge of the truth of what really went down, just of what was told her and the public.

"Monica how was your day? Did you do anything interesting?"

"My day was good. I taught two classes and had my teacher assistant to help me grade some art project. I had to pick up my boys from their after school programs. Then we came home and I prepared dinner and made sure the boys did their homework. I had a very busy day. I miss not having help with the boys. When I lived in Harlem, NY my mom and dad helped me with the boys but living here I lack the help I need working as an art professor."

"I do see that you do have a full plate with the boys and your work.

Maybe you can hire a nanny? That could help you out a lot. The nanny could pick the boys up their after school programs when you can't make it there. She could have dinner really for you and the boys on your busy days."

"That would be nice to have a person like that to help me out on my busy school days. But my budget doesn't permit me to hire a nanny at this moment."

I understand, but I could help you with the funds you need to hire a nanny. I can also help you look for a good candidate to hire."

"Oh no! I could not let you do that. But thank you for the offer. It isn't your responsibility to help me with the boys. Don't want to feel like I am using you, though it would be a huge help for me."

"My sweet friend I insist for you are not using me. I have more than enough for myself and I see my friend in need so I want to take my extra to help her in her area of need. I want you to have a peace of mind. I know what it is like to have too much to do and not have anyone to help you. For when I was a young boy I have to work on my parents dairy farm in the summer and my brothers and sisters were too young to help out on the farm. My parents couldn't afford to hire farm hands so there was lots of work for me to do. I wished back then my parent could have hired some help so I didn't have to work so hard!"

"Oh really? I didn't know you grew up on a farm. Wow you really do know what it means to be busy. If you insist for I don't want to be a bother!"

"Oh no it is not a bother it's a pleasure to help my friend! I can help you look for good candidates tomorrow. I have a few contacts sources I can begin looking into."

"Okay that would be great. I want to Thank You, for that's a huge help to me. You don't really know what this really means to me!"

"You are welcome! I am looking forward to going to BSU home football game with you and the boys on Saturday!"

"We are looking forward to it as well! It will be a fun day for us. It's our first college game we will be attending."

"Really, I used to play college football for Miami back the day."

"Oh wow really, you are more than meets the eye! I enjoyed our talk tonight Josiah. It is so great talking to you. You can call me tomorrow night if you like? But need to go to bed so I can get up early to get the boys ready for school."

"Okay I will call you tomorrow night! Good night Monica and sweet dreams to you."

"Thank you sweetie, good night and sweet dreams to you as well!"

I hung up the phone with a heart full of joy for her voice was still dancing around in my head. Monica was a dream girl that I wanted to make my reality. I have always been busy with my career and didn't have time for a relationship. But the moment I saw her I knew she was the one I had to get to know. No woman has grabbed my attention like she has. If this planet was worth saving it was because of Monica. I knew I needed to go to bed so I could get up early to go through my contacts to help Monica get a new nanny.

I woke up just as the sun rose up over the horizon. I went through university database to find persons who posted their résumé on the college's work force website. I had G.A.S run background checks on possible candidates. After getting the background checks back I sent Monica an email of the possible nanny candidate she should interview.

Meanwhile at GAS 225 there was a National Security video conference with Director Beck and Government Security Officials.

Director Beck being informed by scientist James Johnston on the current situation of the alien invaders decided to call for a video conference with the government security officials who put her in charge of G.A.S. The Secretary of State, Secretary of Defense, Secretary of Homeland Security and a few high rating military officials were in attendance at the Pentagon for the video conference. Director Beck opened the conference briefing by greet the government officials.

"Greetings Mr. Secretary of State, greetings Mrs. Secretary of Home-

land Security, and greetings Ms. Secretary of Defense and greetings to all in attendances today. We have a situation on hand today that you will see described in your briefing packets."

Mr. Benjamin A. Stanford, Secretary of State said, *"Good Morning Director Beck. Thank you for calling this conference for we all have been waiting to hear your agency's progress report."*

Director Beck answered, *"Yes Mr. Secretary, on page three of the briefing packet you will find G.A.S progress report. Our scientists have developed some of the state of art technological devices. Our agents have done great work using these devices in searching to find our out of this world visitors. This brings us to our current situation, the reason for today's briefing."*

Mrs. Julianne Ordaz, Secretary of Homeland Security responded, *"Director Beck, I see your progress. What does this have to do with the safety of our Nation?"*

Director Beck answered, *"Too do all respect Mrs. Secretary, our scientists and field agents are working hard to protect the nation for this unknown threat. They discovered and broke the code of an unknown language. We as a team developed a device that can detect the alien's DNA. The DNA we obtained from quick thinking of one of our field agents which apprehended the alien body. So to answer your question Mrs. Secretary our progress has a lot to do with the safety of our Nation. For the more we learn and develop new tech the more safe our Nation will be!"*

Ms. Marsha Peebles, Secretary of Defense answered, *"Excellent Director Beck! G.A.S has made a lot of progress that goes to make our Nation safer. Your agency kept a major incident from the knowledge of the public with little repercussion. So where do we stand on the search?"*

Nicole said, *"This is what brings us together today in this briefing. G.A.S field agents have done many possible identity sketches, and after a massive search there have been no alien presence on our planet at this moment. Our satellites don't detect alien crafts in earth's orbit. But scientists are developing new high tech devices to* detect their craft. We have reason to believe that the aliens haven't left earth's orbit."

Marsha said to Julianne while look at her, "Homeland Security needs to elevate the terror alert to yellow to keep the public aware of a possible terror attack in case something happen in the near future. We want the lie in place to make it possible to spin the public from the truth."

Julianne responded to Marsha by saying, "I will get Homeland Security directors to initiate a yellow terror alert so the nation is on the lookout for a possible terror attacks. We will tell them we have possible Intel of terrorist cells around the country. We will be able to deny any knowledge of any specific terrorist cell. Just we had the knowledge that could have been a terrorist cell operating somewhere on our soil."

Ms. Beck said, "Great that will help G.A.S a lot. Homeland Security can set this alert by sending out national news reports. Secretary Ordaz G.A.S will contact you if we need more news report to be broadcast."

Julianne said to Nicole, "Homeland Security will be happy to help G.A.S any way we can."

Before the video conference ended the high rating military officers that were in attendance there at the Pentagon said, "Please keep the armed forces informed on the situation and let us know how we can help."

Director Beck said, "G.A.S wants to thank you all for your time today. We will succeed in our mission to keep the Earth safe! We will submit a report to each Secretary so everyone stays inform on the situation at hand."

The video conference briefing end and about an hour after their meeting Homeland Security had broadcast to the national news companies that supplied their local news affiliates with Homeland Security report of a yellow terror alert. So by the evening news the whole country had received the report that G.A.S wanted the nation to have. No one was the wiser of the truth not even the President which his cabinet wanted him to have plausible dependability. If somehow the truth leaked out the President could truthfully deny any knowledge of the truth.

The local Brentwood Texas news channel WBTS Channel 36 Action News gave the task of report the national new broadcast to young reporter Dominik Prince. Dominik was eager to do his first on air anchor spot. The news announcer came over the air waves and said, *"Now a special report from WBTS Channel 36 own Action News Report Dominik Prince."* Dominik sitting at the news anchor desk was waiting for his cue from his camera man. The camera man said, *"Dominik in three, two, one you are on the air."* Dominik at that point began reading the news teleprompter and said, *"Good Evening Ladies and Gentlemen this is a breaking news report from Homeland Security national news broadcast. Homeland Security has issued a **Yellow Level Terror Alert** today. Homeland Security wants the Nation to be watchful of possible terror and report anything strange and out of the ordinary to your local law enforcement departments. Homeland Security believes there maybe terrorist cells station around the country. So please never take the law into your own hands always contact your local law enforcement departments. This has been Dominik Prince with your local WBTS Channel 36 Action News Report."*

As Dominik finished his news report he went to the news employee lounge to wait for his next report. He thought it was strange for all out of the blue that Homeland Security would issue a Yellow Level Terror Alert without setting a lower lever alert in the past months. So He wanted to work a continue story of the alert to see what it was all about. Dominik being the young report didn't like taking things he was told at face value. He believed there was a bigger story that Homeland Security was not telling the public and he wanted to get the whole scoop.

He knew if he could break this news story he would position himself for a big promotion. Dominik want to do his homework and break the news story of the century. So he would start at a place he thought was strange for a small country college town. Dominik knew he could not report news as business as usual anymore they were always a bigger stories that were not being told and he needed to get down to the bottom line of every news story he would be given to report on.

CHAPTER 8

FOR US TO KNOW AND YOU TO NEVER FIND OUT!

Being suspicious of the incident at Albert's club Crowning Around, Dominik wanted to know what was the bigger story. Brentwood being a well nit town everyone in the neighborhood knew everyone and Dominik thought that it was strange that someone would try and rob a crowded club. He wanted to know more about the newest town watering hole Crowning Around and its owner.   Dominik went to the internet to find out any information that it could offer about the comedy club.

Amber Shepard, Dominik news producer saw him sitting there in the news room in deep thought. She said to him, *"What's on your mind? You have really zone out on me here!"* Talking to his producer, he said that he felt that there was something strange about the robbery at the comedy club that he reported on. He said, *"You know Amber there is something that I just can't wrap my mind around. That comedy club robbery has me perplexed! After that night I haven't heard anything else about it."*

Amber said, *"You are right Dominik! I haven't heard anyone mention anything. The local newspaper hasn't run a story about it or an interview with the local police department."*

He looked her in the eye, *"The local police department wasn't there.*

When Byron and I arrived on the scene the state patrol was already there."

Amber gazed over Dominik's shoulder at the computer screen wondered why the Brentwood Law Enforcement wasn't called to the scene. He was doing research on Crowning Around on the club's new website. On the computer screen were pictures of the interior of the comedy club. This caught Amber eye for she have never seen a club like this in the mid-west before. The style seemed to be out of place, which it was a northeastern 40's gangster type of club. It didn't look like a place where a modern Texas cowboy would frequent. She asked him, *"Why would someone build this here?"* Turning around and looking at her he shrugged his shoulders at her to say with his body language I really don't know.

She put her hand on his shoulder and with serious tone in her voice said, *"We need to find out what is to know here. Breaking what is behind this story will launch our careers on the national scene. So keep me informed of what you find, gather the clues and I will help you map it all together so we can know what the bigger story is."*

Dominik knowing that Amber was giving him the green light to chase the facts down of the story that could make or break his career he agreed to do things her way. She encouraged his to do some undercover research by attending a few of the nightly shows at the comedy club. She wanted him to get a scent of the club to see how things are run. Amber advised him to be aware of the security procedure of the club. She felt that running a background check on the club owner was in order. He was new to Brentwood and no one knew much about him.

Amber had a close friend in the Brentwood police department that owed her a favor. She called Detective Kathy Clark to see if she would run a background check on Albert Crown. Detective Clark and Amber were college roommates doing their freshmen year. In a case that Detective Clark was working on when she first join the force Amber run a news story that helped Kathy solve the case which got her promoted to detective.

"Hi Kathy, this is Amber. I am in need of a big favor"

"Hey Amber! How are you doing? How can I help you?"

"I am good, you know me, a busy little bee! I need you to run a check on someone for me."

"Sure, I still owe you that favor. I never like owing a debt anyway. Who is it that you want me to check out?"

"It is the owner of the new comedy club in town, Albert Crown."

"That place is called Crowning Around right?"

"Yea it is."

"Why do you want to do a check on him? He asked you out on a date and you want to see if he has ever been locked up before? I heard he was cutie though."

"No! Girl you are too much, I don't have any time for no man, This busy bee is all about that Honey! Ha ha ha. WBTS ran a news report about an incident that happen at his club awhile back and we want to check out some things out. I wouldn't know if he was cute or not for I never seen him before. I need you to run a check on the guy who gave us an interview at the scene of the incident also."

"I know if he did ask you out you would have known his credit rating already since you are about that Honey busy bee! Ha ha ha. So what's the name of this second guy? So that's two favors you need from me, you will owe me now!"

"You are too funny, not! The second guy is Professor Josiah Lewis. Yes I will be in your debt now!"

"Okay, you mentioned an incident? What was the incident that you are talking about?"

"Oh you didn't hear? It was a robbery on its grand opening night."

"*Really? I never heard about that. I'm not in that department so I wouldn't heard of it. Plus I have been too busy to watch the news.*"

"*First of all what do you mean you are too busy to watch the news? I work too hard producing this news show for you not to watch it! Ha ha ha…. The local police department wasn't called to the scene according to our reporter Dominik Prince. He said when they arrived on the scene the State Patrol was already there.*"

"*Oh really, I believe that club is in city limits. I will check on that as well. That doesn't sound like that would be right. Anything in city limits the local patrol would check it out not the state patrol. Just give me three days to get back with you the information.*"

"*Sure, Thank you for the help!*"

"*Any time friend.*"

After talking to her friend Amber felt there was something strange going that had the state patrol involve instead of the local police department. She gave Dominik money from WBTS News petty cash account so he could go steak out the club that night. They needed to get to the bottom of this story as soon as possible. She told him not to make it look like he was working a story, if there was a bar sit there and have a few drinks and loosen up. Joking she said to him, "*Who know, you may get lucky tonight and meet someone!*" He thought maybe she had already been to Happy Hour and had a few drinks for he never had seen her in such a playful mood before, not knowing that talking with Detective Kathy Clark had brought her back to her college days where it was all full of great memories.

After leaving the news station, Dominik drove across town to his two bedroom apartment to freshen up for a night at the comedy club. Tonight would be a great night to meet someone for all expenses was on WBTS News dime. Mixing business with pleasure wouldn't be a bad thing that cross his mind as he looked for a descent outfit to wear. He read online that Crowning Around wasn't the type of club you come wearing t-shirt, jeans, and cowboy boots. The club website stated that there will be no one permitted to enter the premises without formal wear. Formal wasn't hard to find in his closet for being a TV news reporter he had to wear nice suits on air. After picking the suit he wanted to wear and taking a nice hot shower he was dress to mingle.

Surprised to see a club in a Texas small town with valet parking he took the valet ticket and walked toward the front door to enter the club. There were humongous men standing at the front door checking people's identification as they tried to enter the comedy club making sure they were of a legal age. Albert felt this person was of importance which he didn't have on the night of incident so he hired an undercover G.A.S agent to be his bouncer to make certain no unwanted visitor came in which were aliens. Dominik wonder if the club had a bouncer on the night of the incident.

One of the bouncers at the front door took Dominik ID to check it, looked at his ID and looked back up at Dominik said, *"Hey you are that news reporter Dominik Prince! I have seen you on WBTS News a few times. What brings you here tonight?"* Dominik being a new local celebrity, shock by that anyone really knew his said, *"Yes I am, I have the night off and wanted to have a fun evening and see how the comedy club would be."* Giving him his ID back the bouncer said, *"Have a good time and enjoy the acts."* Feeling lucky that the bouncer didn't say no news reporters allowed shook his head in a way to say thank you and he walked into the club.

Dominik walked up to the hostess Janet Walker to be seated. Looking up from her notepad Janet noticed him standing there waiting to be seated said to him, *"Welcome to Crowning Around where Laughter Isn't Just Fun and Games! But every joke is tested for your entertainment enjoyment! Would you like a table for one or will you be waiting for someone? You can also seat at our bar if you are alone."* Dominik responded *"I am here alone; I would like a seat at the bar.*" Pointing him in the direction of the bar she said to him, *"Enjoy your evening."* He thanked her and walked over to the bar to grab a seat.

Seeing an empty seat at the bar Dominik ask the young lady who was sitting next to it if the seat was taking. With a sweet soft Spanish accent she told him it wasn't taking. Hoping to strike up a conversation with the young lady that he thought was a hottie he set beside her. The bartender asked him what he will be drinking. Dominik responded, *"I like a cola with ice."* As the bartender handed him his cola he looked over at the young lady and said *"I'm Dominik. How are you this evening?"* Smiling at him with a blush on her face she said, *"Hi I am Cecilia. My day had been okay I can't complain. It's nice to meet you Dominik."*

Dominik falling deep into a conversation with Cecilia had almost forgot the main reason why he came to the club. Being bewildered by her voice he needed a second to gather himself and get his thoughts together. Not knowing much about the club he asked her a few questions to see what she knew about the place. *"This is my first time here. Do you come here often?"* Cecilia being intrigued by Dominik's eastern European accent answered his question, *"I have been here a few times. My college professor told me about the place. It is one of the few fun spots in town. The acts are almost as good as the food here."*

"Oh, you are a student at the university. I just graduated not long ago myself from there. What year are you at BSU?"

"I am a freshman. I am an exchange student from Peru, I just been in the country for a few months now. My neighbor Professor Josiah Lewis told me that his good friend Albert Crown was opening up a comedy club and I should check it out when I get a chance."

Know that the name of Cecilia's neighbor sounded familiar he asked her, *"The club owner and your neighbor are friends. Has your neighbor introduced you to his friend?* Asking the bartender for another ice tea she looked at Dominik, *"Yes he did. I met Albert on grand opening night. The house was pack that night. I came with a few friends I met at BSU."* Not knowing she was there that night when he did his report he decided to tell her what he did for a living. *"After I graduated from BSU I got a job at WBTS News as a reporter. So you were here that night when the club got robbed? I came to report the story after it all went down."* Taking a sip of her ice tea Cecilia explained to Dominik how that night was.

"Yes my friends and I was there but we didn't really see anything for we were seated at a table in the front of the club. We got there early to wait in line to get a good table to see Stevie Paige's act. When the robbery went down we didn't see anything but I heard a shot. It didn't sound like a normal gun shot. By the time I looked around my neighbor was escorting the people out of the club."

Dominik just remembering who Cecilia's neighbor was said to her, *"I knew your neighbor sounded familiar. I did the interview with him that night after the robbery. He told WBTS News what happen that night. When you mention his name I was trying to remember if I knew him for his name rang a bell."* Cecilia being somewhat intrigued by him being the reporter who interview Professor Josiah Lewis she decided she would like to talk to him more to get to know him. She asked him. *"Would you like to go to my place after the last comedy act so we could talk more?"* Not thinking she was being forward for he was really liking her as well Dominik said, *"Yes that would be great for I would really like to get to know you."* He knew this would be a good opportunity to see what type of neighborhood Josiah Lewis lived in.

Dominik asked Cecilia did she know how long Albert and Josiah were friends she responded, *"I think Mr. Lewis said Mr. Crown have been friends prior of them both going into the military."* The bartender over hearing their conversation said *"I believe Albert told us that before he went into the Navy he met Josiah who was a college football quarterback at the time."* Dominik asked the bartender *"So they served in the Navy together?"* The bartender said *"No Josiah went in to the Marines after he finished college."* Dominik said *"Oh Really?"* He thought to his self it was strange that two friends who were in two different branches of the military would end up in the same little town.

The comedy club acts had wrapped up the last performance of the evening, Dominik asked Cecilia if she was ready to leave. He was very interested in seeing her neighborhood. Cecilia said, *"Yes we can go to my place for some coffee and dessert so we can talk more"*, for the evening was still young. Dominik gave his valet ticket to the attendant. Cecilia having taking a cab to the club allowed Dominik to drive her home. Pulling into her neighborhood Cecilia pointed out which house was Josiah Lewis to him.

After a few cups of coffee and a couple slices of apple pie, which Cecilia brought from the local baker, Dominik decided to call it a night. He wanted to write down the information that he learned about Albert Crown and Josiah Lewis during the night. Dominik said, *"Cecilia, I had a great night. I have to work early tomorrow. Can I see you tomorrow for a mid-afternoon lunch?"* Cecilia responded, *"I had a great time as well! I am going to BSU first home football game tomorrow afternoon. Maybe you can come over tomorrow evening and I will fix dinner?"* Dominik said, *"That would be great!"*

As he drove home Dominik thought to himself maybe he could spy around Josiah place tomorrow for Josiah just might go to the game also since it was the school's first game of the season. Arriving home he wrote his report on Albert and Josiah to give it to Amber in the Saturday morning meeting.

Kathy faxed the background information about Albert Crown and Josiah Lewis early Saturday morning. Amber walking in the WBTS news room early that morning was surprise to see Kathy fax. Amber taking Dominik's report she told him, *"we will talk later after our morning meeting."* Ending a brief news meeting Amber was eager to go over the information to see if the story was worth pursuing. She moved swiftly to her office avoiding any long conversation with her colleagues that would prolong her anticipation. Sitting down at her desk Amber pulled the multiple page fax from her desk drawer which read.

"Background Check For Albert Crown"

"Full Legal Name: Albert Christopher Crown III"

"Place of Birth: San Francisco, CA"

"Date of Birth: April 21, 1963"

"Branch of Armed Forces: US Navy"

"Highest Military Rank: Lieutenant Junior Grade"

"Military Status: Retired, Honorable Discharged after 20 years of service"

"Criminal Record: Post-Gulf War Service while station at Norfolk Virginia port there were several incidents while on R&R leave, Albert was arrested for disorderly conduct because of bar fights. All charges were eventually dropped"

"Current Occupation: Club Owner, Crowning Around"

"Current Place of Residence: Brentwood Texas"

"Background Check For Josiah Lewis"

"Full Legal Name: Josiah Alexander Lewis Jr"

"Place of Birth: Hot Springs, SD"

"Date of Birth: February 14, 1959"

"Education: University of Miami"

"Branch of Armed Forces: US Marines"

"Highest Military Rank: Captain"

"Military Status: Retired Pilot, Honorable Discharged after 20 plus years of service"

"Criminal Record: None"

*"**Current Occupation:** College Professor"*

*"**Current Place of Residence:** Brentwood Texas"*

*"**Notes:** Josiah received his BS degree in Aerospace Engineering. He won The Heisman Trophy as the Hurricane's quarterback his senior year.*

Reading the fax Amber thought there was something about Albert's past with bar fights. Calling Dominik to come into her office, she wanted to go over the report he gave her that morning. Amber told him that she received the background check on Albert Crown and Josiah Lewis that morning from her detective friend. They went over the fax and his report to see if there was any information in them that was worth investigating. His report stated that Albert and Josiah had different backgrounds, so it appeared strange to them these two would be friends. Josiah was a high school and college football star who chose the US Marines over playing Pro ball. Albert seemed to have a trouble past while in the Navy compared to Josiah clean service record.

Amber said to Dominik, *"There is a story behind why these two guys became friends and both chose to retire from the military and move together to this town. Sure Josiah got a job teaching BSU, but why did Albert decided to move here and open up a comedy club?"* Dominik responded to her, *"You know Amber that's what has me puzzled! Do they have this great friendship that they desire to live near each other? Or is there some other underline reason why they moved here?"* She said, *"So according to your report the club security was tight?"* Lifting his head up from the notes that he was writing Dominik said, *"Yes the security presence was highly enforced unlike the night of the robbery. I don't remember seeing any security other than the State Patrol."*

Wondering how he gathered his information she said to him, *"So tell me did you get lucky last night? Did you meet the future Mrs. Prince?"* With a smile on her face she broke out in a huge laugh. Having a large grin and blush on his face he spoke with a soft voice, *"Yes I met someone, a neighbor of Josiah Lewis but I wouldn't go as far to say the future Mrs. Prince! We have a dinner date this evening. While she at BSU's home football game this afternoon I going to spy around Josiah's neighborhood to see if I can gather some more clues."* Trying to hold back the tears because of her laughter she spoke with a sarcastic tone *"Make sure you don't do anything to get yourself arrested for we don't have enough money in our petty cash account to pay bail!"* Being the brunt of her joking Dominik asked *"Will there be anything else? If not I have some work to finish at my desk before I left today."* Not having any more to say Amber told him that would be all for today.

Finishing up the paper work of a local news story that he had be assign to report about the annual Brentwood Cook Off Festival Dominik packed up his briefcase to leave the office for the weekend. It was early afternoon knowing that the game was underway Dominik decided to drive over to Cecilia neighborhood. He felt hopeful that there would be a good chance that Professor Lewis would not be home being that it was Brentwood State University first home football game. He knew that he was a former college quarterback the game was still in his blood and he wouldn't miss a chance to go to a game.

Arriving at Westchester Heights Dominik parked across the street from Professor Lewis from subdivision. He didn't see a car in Josiah's driveway when he walked up to house, wanting to know if he was home Dominik walked up to the garage door to peep through the glass. Josiah's SUV wasn't in the garage for he left to go to the game two hours before Dominik arrived at his house. Seeing that Josiah wasn't home Dominik jumped the fence to the backyard. Picking the lock to the back door he entered the kitchen to look around to see what he could find. Looking like a thief in the night with his black hood that covered his face and black leather gloves not to leave finger prints because Dominik took Amber jokes to heart. Carefully searching through the house he came to Josiah's home office and began to pick the lock on Josiah's desk drawer. Taking just seconds to pick the locks being a skilled lock picker from his younger days of running with a Ukrainian street gang.

As Dominik searched through the desk he flipped the papers one by one trying to find anything that he would use to make scents of the club robbery. He felt deep in his heart that Josiah was hiding some important detailing to the robbery. But he found nothing of importance that he sought. All that was in Josiah's desk was his lecture notes. Looking around the room Dominik thought to himself maybe there was a hidden safe. He said if this was a movie there would be a hidden safe in the wall hiding behind a picture but Josiah had olny pictures on his office wall that was *The Heisman Trophy pose photo*. Dominik had no idea that Josiah had a hologram of a wall on the right side of his office behind his *The Heisman Trophy pose photo* .

Getting up from the desk chair, walking toward the right side of the room where there was a medium size filing cabinet he tripped. Trying to catch his balance he place one hand on the cabinet and the wall beside the cabinet. To his surprise his hand went straight through the wall. The wall had no hole where is hand was but he could not see his hand. He took his hand out of the wall and there was no hole in the wall where his hand went through. Puzzle by what just happen he thought how could this be? He never saw anything like this before for the tech was of a high technology.

He placed his hand back into the wall curious about what was going on. His hand and whole arm went through the wall but he felt nothing. So placing both arms in the wall to see what would happen, he started to move his arms around to see if he could feel anything. Dominik did not know that the whole right side wall was a hologram. Dominik seeing that nothing happen when he put his arms through the wall it should be okay to place his head through the wall as well. But a safety device flashed a bright light that instantly blinded Dominik for a few minutes because he was not wearing the protective shades that was in Josiah desk draw that looked like an ordinary pair of sunglasses. Determine not to let the loss of his sight keep him from getting behind the mystery of the wall that was no wall he walked through the wall and knelt to gather his self. It took several minutes for his sight to slowly return. He started to see things in the extension of the room behind the hologram wall a little blurry.

After rubbing his eyes the whole time he was kneeling his sight came back good enough to see what was in the room. He looked behind him and there was no wall. Looking above his head he saw the device that was portraying a wall on the other side of the room. There were gun cabinets on the two side walls full with rifles and automatic assault weapons. Not really interested in Josiah collection of weapons for that wasn't strange for a military man. He looked at the back wall which a large safe was protruding from it. Now Dominik thought there must be something very important in a safe that was hiding in a hidden room behind a fake wall.

Putting out his PDA he searched the internet on how to crack a safe. To his surprise the search bought up a website that had detail info on safe cracking for beginners. Dominik wished that he had learned the safe cracking skill while he was in the gang because he spent thirty minute without any success. Scrolling through several of the website pages it told him now that he learned the skills of a beginner safe cracker that he would not crack one safe for it would take more than being a beginner. The site recommended that he buy its safe cracking info for $49.99.

Feeling like he was robbed of his time, he was determined to open the safe with the info that he got from that site. Turning the dials on the safe it was with a stroke of luck that the safe door popped open as if the safe gods were tired of seeing him struggle. He looked in to the safe and saw a large scroll; he partly unrolled it and saw a design of something that he didn't understand at first glance. Knowing it was getting late in the afternoon and the game should be about over and didn't want to be caught in the house he left the house in a hurry. He left the safe door open being in a rush. Running out the kitchen door he stop at the backyard fence to peep over it to see if anyone was there so he would not get caught. Not seeing anybody he climbed over the fence and walked quickly to his car. He needed to meet Cecilia in a few hours at her home for dinner so he drove home to hide the scroll that was in the safe. He wanted to take a better look at it later after his dinner date.

Driving across town Dominik noticed a dark cloud in the sky. Arriving home he ran into his apartment to put the large scroll in the back of his closet. Just as he hid the large scroll his phone rang. He picked it up wondering who it was. He said *"Hello."* Amber answered, *"Hi Dominik, it's Amber. There has been an incident at the university. WBTS needs you to go at once to do live coverage."* Dominik being caught off guard said, *"I will meet Byron there in ten minutes."* Amber responded *"Good for Byron is on his way from the station now. Meet him outside the football stadium."* He hung up the phone wanting to know if Cecilia was alright so he dialed her number. She didn't answer her home phone so he left a message on her answering machine saying he would be a little late for their dinner date because he had to cover a break-ing story at the university.

He left home and made his way to Santa Ana Stadium on the Brentwood State University campus. He walked up to his camera man Byron who was sitting in the WBTS news van. After he greeted him he asked Byron did he know what was going on. Byron told him that he wasn't sure, but what he did know there were some shootings and some people may be injured. While Byron was setting up the camera equipment Dominik went to investigate the news scene. Horrified by the thought of what happen he said to his self who could do this. Walking back to where Byron was setting up Dominik fell to his knees because the thought was too great for him to comprehend. As he did his live report from the massacre at Santa Ana Stadium all he could think was how Cecilia was, for she told him the night before that she was going to the game.

JOSIAH LEWIS STARTED HIS WEEKEND

I woke with Monica on my mind so I called her to see how she was doing. I push the speed dial button to call her. When she picked up the phone I said *"Good Morning Dear how are you doing today?"*

She replied, *"Good Morning Sweetie Pie, I am well! Thank you for asking. How are you?"*

"You are very welcome! I am great. Hearing your voice has started my day off right" I said to her. I told her that the game starts around noon so I should be there about eleven o'clock to pick her and the boys up to go to the game. Monica said that would be good and they were looking forward to the game.

After I got off the phone I set out the outfit I was going to wear. Jeans and a nice BSU football jersey were in order. This would be the first college football game I would attend since I was in college over twenty years ago. A break was in order for this G.A.S UFO agent for chasing down Ploutcraft and the Varldoion aliens. I have been looking forward to spending time Monica and her sons. But my secret life she was not allowed to know. I didn't like that part of my life she could not find out about for it felt like I was lying to her. It was locked up tight like the blueprints that I have in my office safe.

My father didn't know about my secret life and we are

very close for I talked to him about everything. I told my dad about Monica and how we met. He laughed at me and said *"Son when I met your mom I knew she was the only one for me, and I chased her for four months before she knew I was alive."* He went onto tell how he went on his campaign to sweep her of her feet. He said but he treated her with respect and they didn't have their first kiss until their wedding night. *"The youths of today would have their tongues all down each other throats the first minute they meet,"* he would say to me as we talked. Some would call my dad old fashion but I agreed with his way so for that fact I must be old fashion as well.

I took my dad's advice and made my campaign to woo Monica off her feet so she would fall deeply in love with me. Today I would put my campaign in to play and start to get to know Monica and her three sons, Robert Jr., Antonio, and Samuel. Monica told me that her youngest son Samuel has begun to be captivated by football. He could sit in front of the TV on a Sunday afternoon and you wouldn't hear a word from him until the games has gone off. So this game this afternoon will be straight up his alley. Building a friendship with these three young men will be my key to winning Monica's affections. But I am sincere in building a friendship with her sons though for I am not looking to use them to get with their mother. My heart motives are pure, I am my father's son and he is the purest motive person I know.

Being dress casually shaped, it was about time to leave and pick up Monica and her sons for the game. I pulled out of the garage and drove down the street heading out the neighborhood. The Tosba Calvary-Cross special features were hidden in plain sight. The only one I ever had in the SUV was Albert, so I had to be extra careful not to accidentally push buttons of the special features. I arrived at the address Monica gave me. It took about eighteen minutes from my place. The GPS said her place was about twenty minutes from my parking lot on campus. But with the game day traffic the drive probably would be around forty five minutes. That would leave just enough time to get our seats if we leave right away. Hopefully everyone will be ready to go now that I am here. I walked up to the door and rang the doorbell, Robert Jr. answered the door and said his mom said to come in and she will be ready in a few minute. I could come in and have a seat, make myself at home.

She made her way downstairs, the beautifulness which she was took my breath away. The smile that she carried on her face lit up the room where I was sitting like a bright morning sun shine. Her long dark silky hair had me captivated for I was a sucker for a beautiful woman with long hair. The short time that I have known her, this was the first time I seen her real smile. Dressed in her dressy casual outfit she was a breath of fresh air. She told me the boys and her were ready to go. They didn't want to be late to the game especially Samuel, for he couldn't sleep all night. The excitement for the outing had them ready for a great time. We walked to the Tosba Calvary-Cross, being a gentleman I open the SUV's doors for everyone when they were all settled in with the seatbelts fasten I drove off. With my GPS set to give me perfect direction to the parking lot with the least traffic we were on our way to the game.

Arriving with time to spare we stop at the vendor to get the perfect snacks to help us enjoy the game. The seats were perfect just far back enough to see the whole field; it was a plus that Monica was seated next to me, I was on cloud nine. I don't know if she noticed the smile on my face the whole time we seated there together. I looked over at Samuel and he was enjoying his cola and eating a hot dog looking forward to the game's kickoff. The away team won the coin toss and decided to get the ball first. BSU chose the side of the football field they wanted to defend. My mind was totally carefree at that moment just being with Monica and her sons. At that moment my secret life was forgot about, for if someone would have called me Special Agent Lewis. I would have said who?

The first quarter was very exciting, though BSU were down by seven points. Gainesville University Golden Razorbacks came to play. Brentwood State University Fighting Groundhogs need to pick up their game play. If I was not enjoying Monica's company I would have gone down to the sideline and show the BSU coaches how they needed to coach the talent they had. But by the second quarter the BSU coaches began to call the correct plays that put their players in the right places to make plays. I began to have a flash back to my high school football championship game. I haven't thought about that game in years, but the Fighting Groundhogs started to play more like wild hogs than little groundhogs. I never understood how BSU came up with the mascot Fighting Groundhogs. Maybe it was that we were a small college in a small town so they chose a humble small mascot.

It was almost halftime and Antonio asked if he could go used the restroom for he had drank one too many soda pops. So I told Monica I would take the boys to the restroom, she decided to come with us. She could take a restroom break as well. Just as we were getting out of our seats BSU's quarterback Billy Jackson threw a deep bomb to his receiver Jonny Mills for a Touchdown. That tied the game up at fourteen each. I thought wow we almost missed the best play of the whole game so far.

Monica looked at me began to say with excitement, *"Josiah that how you throw a deep pass! I could only imagine when you were a college quarterback you threw a pretty ball like that."*

I replied, *"My Dear I can still throw a pretty pass, but way better than these young kids in this game today."*

She started to laugh; she said *"You didn't know that I knew that you played quarterback in college? I have been doing my homework on you. I like what I saw and see."*

I said *"I see you are doing your homework for I never got the chance to tell you about my college quarterback days."* I was a little shocked that she went to the internet to find out about my past. As that touchdown play has bought the game to halftime we walked the boys to the restroom.

Waiting on the boys to finish up in the restroom I could hear BSU marching band music through the stadium restroom doors. The stadium crowd was cheering as the Fighting Ground-hogs Marchers played. Half-time was as good as the game at BSU because the fans always looked forward to the playing of the Marching Groundhogs.

It became silent in the stadium though the band's half-time section wasn't over. As I waited on the boys I wondered what was going on so I peeked out the restroom door. At first I didn't notice anything out of the ordinary that would raise alarm. As the boys and I walked out the restroom Monica was coming out of the ladies' room. We stopped by the vendor's booth before heading back to our seats to see if Robert Jr., Antonio, and Samuel wanted anything.

I started to notice people rushing pass us. Out of no-where I began to hear loud noise. I told Monica to stay there at the vendor with the boys while I went to check things out. I went to the nearest aisle way opening to see what was going on. I came to the edge of the opening and looked on the field and saw all the band members lying on the field of the stadium. I thought that was strange, than I looked around and notice no one on the field was standing around. Wearing my G.A.S sunglasses that double as binoculars; Tom and the folks in the lab fitted the glasses to help you notice alien signature activity. As I looked through the sunglasses binocular feature I saw three gunmen standing on the sideline holding automatic weapons. Switching on the alien signature activity feature on the glasses I could see that the gunmen were under alien mind control.

Immediately I called Albert and the G.A.S team to tell them I needed them here at once for we had a situation with alien mind control and shots been fired. We needed to take control of the situation quickly. Walking quickly back to Monica and the boys I told them that there were gunmen on the field and I wanted to get them to safety. Before I could get them to parking lot there were reporters and Brentwood city police on the scene. G.A.S officials disguised as U.S. Marshals got to the stadium once I reached the SUV.

I drove Monica and her boys to their home quickly as possible. She started to question me what was going on. *"Josiah, what was going on at the stadium? You said there were gunmen on the field? Why were they there shooting?"*

I tried to answer her question without giving away G.A.S secret. *"Yes Monica I noticed people moving quickly passed us when we were at the hot dog vendor. I went to see what was the loud noise was that I heard and someone I stopped to ask what was going on told me that there were three men on the field shooting all the band members. That's when I came back to get y'all so we could get to safety. I don't know why they were at BSU shooting but the government has an amber alert for terror attack for a little bit. I can't say they were terrorists but they could have been."*

She looked at me and said, *"Really? You think we have terrorists here in Brentwood Texas? We just a small college town! Why would terrorists attack here? We are not important to anyone!"*

I answer her, *"Dear anything is possible these days! Maybe Brentwood was an easy target for people like you and I wouldn't expect terrorists to attack so security would not be a big present at events. My military background if I was a terrorist that's where I would want to attack. It's sad that the real terrorists would have that same thought! I only lived here for a short time but I believe because Brentwood and BSU are strong communities we will pull together to get through this and bounce back tighter than we were before all of this happen!"*

Monica's boys had a sad face on them for the shooters ruin their great day of college football. Monica responded, *"I* know the boys are upset especially lil Sammy who been looking for-ward to this day for a little while now. We won't let those terrorists ruin what we have here in Brentwood! We as a community will come together. I want to go to church tomorrow to pray for our community will you come with us?"

I answered, "Sure I will go to church with you tomorrow! If you like I can pick y'all up and we can arrive there together." It has been a long while since I been to a church service but for her I would go anywhere!

Monica said, "Good, we will be really by nine o'clock A.M. for the service starts at ten and I want to be there a little early."

By the time she said that we reach her home, I said, "I am sorry our day was cut short, I look forward to church tomorrow!"

Monica hugged me, looking me in the eye asked, "Josiah would you like to come in for a little bit?"

The inner man wanted to say yes but my real job wouldn't let me do so. I said to her, "I would love too but there are some things back on campus I really need to check on, the university has me as point of contact if they are in need of anything in situ-ations like this. But tomorrow morning I am totally free for church."

She said, "I understand be careful Sweetie. Call me later when you get home tonight."

I told her that I would. Leaving Monica's place I drove back to campus to see how I could help G.A.S figure out what happen there. I called Albert to see if he was at the stadium. "Hey Al I am on my way back from dropping Monica and her sons at her place. Did you make it to the stadium yet?

The funny man that Albert thought he was said, "Jose I been here before you flew cross the planet to drop off the mother of Josiah The Third and his big brothers. I am about business and hand-ling things behind the scene."

I couldn't let Albert crack on me without me having a witty come back. *"Man don't be jealous because there is a woman out there who want to have my kids and the only woman you had a chance to be with was from another planet but your two gun wheeling self shot and killed her before you could say can I buy you a drink!"*

Albert said with a lite laugh in his voice, *"Josiah I turn down more women on a nightly basis than Wilt Chamberlain ever had but enough about my love life. When you get to campus let us control the situation from the local law enforcement."*

I told Albert to make sure he turns on his face descrambler so no one notice who he was. The face descrambler was a device developed by G.A.S lab techs which use a hologram image to disguise an agent's face so the agent could work undercover.

I parked the Tosba Calvary-Cross in the campus parking deck and walked to the nearest building to change into my US Marshal's disguise and turned on my face descrambler. I called Albert to let him know I was on campus. He gave me a update of what was going on at the stadium. Someone in the stadium called the Brentwood Police Department when the shooters began shooting on the field. BPD assigned Detective Kathy Clark to the case. When Albert arrived on the scene she and her fellow officers were there doing their investigations. By that time G.A.S got to the stadium to set up our US Marshal portable base. G.A.S knew that situation had alien involvement so it was important to get BPD and Detective Kathy Clark and her fellow officers off of the case.

Agent Crown walked up to Detective Kathy Clark and flashed his US Marshal badge and said he was Agent Mal Brown the Department of the US Marshal were taking over the case and they need to leave and stop messing up his crime scene. He told her any information that BPD had gathered was now property of the US Marshal and they were turn it over to him or his partner.

He told her my name was Agent Isaiah Blues. Detective Clark walked away very upset because US Marshal were pushing her off her first really big case in years. Things like this don't happen in Brentwood.

Detective Clark called her supervisor at BPD to see what was going on. Steaming with every ringtone of her cell phone and by the time her supervisor answered the phone Detective Clark could have boiled a dozen eggs!

"Captain Washfield I was just told by some dude supposedly from the US Marshal that we were to stop our investigation and turn everything we collected over to them. What is going on here?"

He answer her, *"Detective Clark, I just received a call from the US Marshal office in Washington D.C., I was told that their office were sending officers who were in the state of Texas investigating terrorist activity to investigate the shooting at BSU for they believe it's terrorist related. They will take over from where you were in your investigation and you or your fellow officers were not to speak to anyone about the information you have collected so you won't face federal charge of instruction of justice."*

She being hotter than a train steam engine said before she blew her top, *"Capt., instruction of justice for doing my job! I do what you say but I am not happy with this. I am just letting you know right now! I need a few days of leave to calm myself down; for I believe the next criminal I see will seriously get hurt and I don't care if all he is doing is jay-walking!"*

Captain Washfield said to her, *"Det., I will have none of that talk for it's out of our hands. But you go take a few days off to calm down before you do something that I have to bring charges up on you for!"*

Neither Captain Washfield nor Detective Kathy Clark knew that the official of the US Marshal Office in Washington D.C. that called the BPD was no other than G.A.S Director Nicole Beck. I caught up with Albert who was going as US Marshal Mal

Brown. He slipped me my US Marshal badge that came from G.A.S headquarters. He informed me that my cover was US Marshal Isaiah Blues. We started to talk to each other using our undercover identities just in case there were non-G.A.S personnel around listening. Mal informed me about the case at hand.

He said, *"Isaiah, we have the three shooters in custody. We are starting the interrogations. You might want to assign an agent to the press or handle it yourself for your friend Reporter Dominik Prince is there with the WBTS news crew. I have assigned agents to crowd control. We have gathered the evidence that the BPD missed. The department has begun analyzing it."*

I said, *"Mal he no more my friend than yours! But I'll go handle that situation quickly and come back to help with the interrogations."*

I located the WBTS news team. Dominik was recording a news report of the situation in the stadium. I walked up to him where they had set up outside of the stadium and introduce myself as US Marshal Isaiah Blues. I told him that the US Marshal Office had everything under control and we needed him and WBTS news crew to let everyone know that everything is under control and once all the evidence been gathered there will be an official report to the press. Dominik asked me could I give him something unofficial. I told him unofficial there were shoots fired by multiple gunmen but we are not sure on the total count at this point. At least one die and multiple people are injured. The EMTs are helping the injured and taking them to the local hospital. We have some suspects in custody but investigating if the suspects acted alone.

I gave them a bone to chew on to help G.A.S spin the situation later to cloud the evidences from alien involvement. After talking to the WBTS news crew I went back to the area where G.A.S was interrogating the shooting suspects. Albert was interrogating a suspect as I walked into the room. We needed to see what the suspect remembered so we decided to do good cop bad cop. Of course Albert had to be the bad cop I don't know how he did it without cracking both of us up. We knew what went down and how it went down from the evidence reading the report that the G.A.S analysis took. We use this technique to see if any of the suspects had any recognition of what they have done that day.

Each shooter wanted to know why they were in custody. They claimed not to know why they were being handled by the US Marshal. They remember waking up that morning and getting ready to go to the football game. Arriving at the game but anything after the first quarter was blacked out until coming to in the custody of the US Marshals. This was the case for each suspect. We showed each suspect the stadium footage of them shooting the band members and the people standing on the sidelines. Each suspect said that couldn't be them for they didn't remember none of that; that footage had to be Hollywood camera tricks or some kind of special effects.

Albert being the big bad US Marshal Mal Brown grabbed the suspects by their shirt collars and said, "*This footage is you dirt bag and it's no special effect or camera trick! You better tell us why you came to this game to kill all these people before I pistol whip you until the cows come home!*"

I said, "*You better tell him something for there are no cows allowed in city limits and he's too wild for me to keep under control for just the other day he beat the cactus juice out of a suspect for pick pocketing at a county fair!*"

We did this act for each suspect and on each one it had the same effect,too afraid to try to remember anything. The G.A.S extraction team collected every piece of evidence and search the remains of the victims for alien evidences then release them to the local coroner department, per G.A.S protocol procedures, so they could process the remains. The extraction team sedated the suspects and took them to a facility that G.A.S had erected in the Texas desert for situation just like this.

From the evidence we collected G.A.S had an understanding of what happen this afternoon. They had planned an attack on Brentwood I can only assume for what happen in Albert's club. We knew that they had mind control abilities but we had no idea they abilities included taking control of a person mind and have them do whatever they wanted them to do. The person who they controlled would have no recognition of being controlled nor doing what they were made to do. Just a whole laps of time was left after being release from the mind control. We knew the suspects were just victims but we just could not let them walk free after world had seen what they did.

It was up to G.A.S to spin them as part of a terror group and let the world know that the federal law enforcement had each suspect in custody. The media was inform in an official press release of each suspect and they charges. The media was given a spin of the event to tell the public. G.A.S turned the suspects over to federal courts and arranged the judgment for each suspect was that they had a brief period of insanity. They would be sentence to life in a country club halfway house with no contact with their family as part of their punishment. After a period of time when the public has forgot about them they be place in a witness protection and told not to go back to their hometown or contact family members for their own well being.

Knowing what powers that Varldoionains were capable of I felt it was more of priority to find them and solve the immediate danger of an invasion. It was late and called Monica to let her know I was still on campus in my office. She told me she was worry for it been awhile since she heard from me. Asked me how was things on campus, I told her that all US Marshals and TV Reporters has left campus and we could lock up campus and go home. Told her I was a little tired but I would be ready for church in the morning. She said to me that she was glad to know I was well and looked forward to church in the morning with me. After hanging up the phone I walked to the parking deck where I parked the SUV.

Driving home I thought how nice this day should have been; how crazy this day got and how the life of G.A.S UFO Special Agent would never be normal no matter how much I pretend it would be. Pulling up the driveway I had a strange feeling but didn't know why. When I first arrived home and got out the SUV in the garage I saw nothing out of the norm. As I walked to the kitchen to get a drink of apple juice I saw the back door in the kitchen was open. I knew I didn't leave the door that way for left through the garage and doors were locked. Curious about why the back door was unlocked I went to investigate. I didn't notice anything out of the norm about the door being unlocked. Because it was getting late I decided to just lock the door and go to bed.

It was early Sunday morning and I needed to pick up Monica and the kids for church then hunt down the Varldoionains before they do anything like yesterday again. When I arrived at Monica's place they were ready so we drove to church. Pulling up to Greater Apostolic Saints, which Monica was a member, the building caught my eye. The stained glass windows and the church steeple gave me that old time church feeling. I wasn't sure what to expect from the service for I haven't been to church in years. If Monica never asked me to come with her I wouldn't have come to Greater Apostolic Saints. I believe in a greater power but never felt the need of church.

We found our seats in the second roll of the church pew so we waited for the beginning of the service. After a few church hymns Bishop Tracy Jackson walked up to the pulpit and started her sermon. *"Welcome everyone; I know we had a sad moment yesterday with the BSU shooting. We pray that God will blessed all the families that lost love ones yesterday. I know He is able to help them deal with the lost. Turn to Romans 8:35 Who shall separate us from the love of Christ? Shall tribulation, or distress, or persecution, or famine, or nakedness, or peril, or sword? Romans 8:38 – 39 says*

For I am persuaded that neither death nor life, nor angels nor princi-
palities nor powers, nor things present nor things to come, nor height
nor depth, nor any other created thing, shall be able to separate us
from the love of God which is in Christ Jesus our Lord."

When she read those verses I was wondering what she
was trying to say. I never thought about the love of God before
Bishop Tracy began to preach. It was a foreign idea until yesterday. I had no need of God in my life was my thought then the
shooting yesterday happen and Monica and the boys could got
hurt. At this moment in church I knew we all need God looking
over us all. For what if God wasn't looking over us and Monica
and the boys were killed in the shooting I wouldn't have for-
gave myself for bringing them to the game and not stopping the
aliens in time. As Bishop Tracy continued to preach her sermon
I knew I had a strange look on my face by what she continued to
say.

"Church I tell you today who is he that condemns? Wasn't it
Christ who died and therefore has risen from the dead! Jesus is at the
Right hand of our father God making intercession for us all. So what
creature from this planet or another, from this realm or another can
separate us all from the Love of Christ, the Holy One of God! Many
people believe in ET but not even ET can keep you from God's love.
In my opinion demons are more real than ET and demons can't stop
God's love from getting to you! So in closing church I say yesterday
events being bad as they were will not keep the Love of Christ from us.
Yes we shall mourn for a season but I say only a short season and be-
cause His Love we will grow closer and stronger as a community!"

Her message truly had me thinking I need God in my life.
She had no idea how real ET really was for they were the cause
of yesterday's event. But when she mention aliens in her sermon
it had me dumbfounded for the Spirit of God knew all things
we are dealing with. I renewed a love for God that I had as a
little child. After service Monica introduced me to Bishop Jackson and I told her that her sermon had me to change my mind

about God and His love for me. She smiled at me and took my hands and began to pray for me so God could continue to work on my heart that would grow in Him. Monica invited me over to her place to eat lunch with her and the boys, being hungry I accepted.

Monica was a great cook; I could not eat another bite for I was stuffed like a thanksgiving turkey. It was getting late in the afternoon, Albert sent me a text message to see what I was doing. I texted him back and told him I was spending time with Monica and the boys. He messaged me back saying he knew I was having fun but we needed to get some work done. I was enjoying myself and didn't want Albert to be right but I knew he was. I told Monica thank you for lunch and I enjoyed being with them today but I had to run because I had to complete some class work for the coming week. She told me to call her later this evening when I got a chance and I told her I would. Driving home to change out of my church clothes I called Albert. I told him I was driving home to change my clothes and I will meet him at his club.

Getting home I parked in the driveway; I unlocked the front door and went up the stairs to my bedroom. Had put on some causal clothes I walked back down stairs to my office to get the Sleep Maker 2000 that I put in my office safe. As I came close to office down the front hallway I saw lights flashing. I moved quickly to the office to find out why the lights were flashing. When I walk into the room I took a quick glance to see what was happening. Something was out of place there was no wall where the hologram of a wall should have been! I looked in the room that the hologram of a wall was hiding to see if anything was missing. At once I notice the safe was cracked open so investigated the break in. I called Albert immediately and told him I had a break in and him and the G.A.S investigating team needed to come to my house disguise as Brentwood City Police officers so that my neighbors wouldn't know who they really were.

I reviewed the surveillance footage of the hidden cameras that I had in the house. I showed a masked man in black coming through the back door in the kitchen the day before while I was at the BSU football game. He walked in the kitchen looking for something but takes nothing from there. He finds his way to my office and went through my desk after he picks the lock on the draws. Searching through the draws he found nothing. According to the footage he stumbles through the hologram of the wall which he began looking around the hidden room. He saw the safe. I prayed; *"Oh no God, please don't let the blue prints been taken!"* As I watched all the footage Albert had arrived at my place. The investigating team disguised as BCPD arrived minutes after Albert did.

After investigating the scene I realized the robber took only the blue prints, it appears that's all he was looking for. I showed the team and Albert the footage and told them that the robber took the very important alien blue prints. The investigate team went to my neighbors dressed as BCPD and asked them did they see any one strange yesterday near Professor Lewis home. Several neighbors told the team that they saw a foreign looking young man dressed in all black walking their neighborhood yesterday afternoon. A neighbor at the edge of the subdivision said a man walked out the subdivision with something in his hands that looked like a long round cylinder and got in a dark late model sports car.

The team took all the information and evidence they gathered back to GAS 225. They gave the description of the man in black that the neighbors described to Agent Awesome Blossum so she could draw a sketch of the suspect in black. It was very important that these blue prints be found at once that G.A.S cover would not be exposed. The last thing I needed was that this info all over the media and GAS 225 be found like other top secret government bases. It was not going to happen on my watch.

As I was certain this secret was going with me to my grave. We had leads and there were not many foreign young looking men driving dark late model sports cars in Brentwood which has knowledge of me and where I live. So he will be found in the next day or two. First thing in the morning I would go to the base to file my report and get a sketch of the robber from Agent Awesome. Albert and I will hunt down the suspect and the aliens to put a stop to this conflict.

CHAPTER 9

CAUGHT RED, BLACK, AND BLUE HANDED!

I was up early being unable to sleep all night with this anxious feeling in my gut! I started to prepare my report in my home office of the break in. It would be a few hours before I could pick up Albert and go to the base. I had an idea of the robber's identity but I want to see Awesome's sketch. At that very moment I looked out my office window I saw a dark navy blue Aston Martin in my neighbor Cecilia Martinez's driveway that I have never seen there before. I took out my camera and took a few pictures of the car. I open my desk draw and grabbed my G.A.S issued tracker bug gun. I opened the window and aimed the tracker laser sight onto the back bumper of the Aston Martin. As I shoot the tracker bug on the back bumper of the sports car the bug blended to the color of the car so it would be detected.

It was time to drive across town to pick up Albert to go to GAS 225 to start a long day of investigation. I uploaded my report and the Aston Martin pictures and tracker link information into my PDA. I hopped in the Tosba Calvary-Cross. The small town traffic was light because the sun wasn't up yet. It took me no time to arrive at Albert's place. I called Albert to let him know I was outside.

"You know Josiah, I'll be glad when we find these crazy aliens for I don't care for these early mornings!"

"Albert you should be used to these early mornings coming from the Navy!"

"Yea Captain, but I'm not in the Navy anymore plus I need my beauty sleep after long nights at the comedy club. Four hours of sleep don't work for me."

"Lieutenant that's the price you pay for laughing and partying all night long!"

"So Jo Lew you have jokes now, I guess I have to book you at Crowning Around to see how well this stand-up act does in front of a real audience!"

"Al Crow you know I would kill it if you did! Ha Ha Ha"

"Captain, keep your two day jobs and leave the night gig to the real comedians before I tell you it's time for you to go Beddy Bye! Ha Ha Ha"

After we had a few laughs with each other we arrived at GAS 225. Pulling into the base Nicky Jones greeted us as usual. I was anxious to get to our office so we could process the information we gathered. When I walked through the office door Agent Awesome was waiting at my desk to give me the sketch she had drawn. I was so happy to see her sitting there for I want see who this person might be. Agent Awesome said she thinks the suspect looks familiar but couldn't place his face. I looked at the sketch and I also thought the person looked familiar.

Albert said he had seen the suspect before. I agreed with Albert and said so did I. Albert played an old video of a news clip of me doing an interview of what happen the night of the grand opening of Crowning Around. Albert said *"Josiah, this is your suspect! He was interviewing you!"* I said that's Dominik Prince the WBTS beat reporter. Why was this guy in my house? How did he learn where I lived? These questions were on the front of my mind.

I logged into my computer to upload the tracker data of the Aston Martin that was in my neighbor Cecilia Martinez's driveway so we could keep an eye on its whereabouts. The global position data system placed the Aston Martin in the WBTS News Station while we were at base. Albert said *"If this is Dominik Prince's Aston Martin. What is he doing at your neighbor's house?"*

I said *"Albert that's a great question, especially that early in the morning! I wonder if has been back to your club since this interview?"*

Albert said, *"Let me go to my desk to log on to my computer so I can tap into my club's surveillance cameras."*

"You can do that from here?" I asked.

He said, *"Yeah, I installed software that allows me to log on to it from anywhere. Plus a face recognition program that will save us time on the search so we don't have to sit here to look through every last second of data."*

Awesome said *"Wow that's neat I didn't know you could do that!"*

Responding to her Albert smiled, *"That's the least of what I can do. It is program to recognize a person face that walks in the door that I deem a threat to Crowning Around so it can info me at once so security can remove them from the club!"*

I was assuming James and Tom gave Albert the equipment to use in the club after that night's incident. That equipment sounded a little more expensive out of Al's pay rate. At least James or Tom helped him install it. Albert and I don't belong to the nerdy geek team. If James and Tom had job opens in their science lab they wouldn't hire us! But I was curious about what he would find. As that thought entered my head Al yelled

"It's finished! It has something!"

I said *"What is it?"*

Albert said, *"It is dated the night before the BSU attack."*

So I walked over to Al's desk to view the footage. The video clip was of Dominik walking over to the bar of the club and starting to talk to a female who was at the bar. When I saw her face I yelled, *"That's my neighbor Cecilia Martinez! Who is also a student in one of my classes."*

Albert said *"what the heck!"*

I asked him did the footage come with sound?

Responding he said, *"What kinda spy would I be if it didn't!"*

I told him that he wasn't a spy but was an UFO agent!

"You and your jokes! How many times do I need to tell you that you ain't funny?" He responded. He turned the sound up on his computer. As I listened to the video Dominik was asking Cecilia questions about Albert and I. He was doing the reporter thing like he was trying to write a news report about us. He had Cecilia to spill her guts about the little she knew about us.

At the end of the surveillance footage she asked him back to her place. I can only assume she showed him my house when they arrived at her home. That would explain how he knew where I lived.

I walked up to Director Beck office door and knocked on it. She told me to enter. I explain to her what we discover about the break in of my place and who the suspect was Dominik Prince of WBTS. I told her I had a plan to recover the blueprints. She asked me what she could do to help with my plans. I said I needed a few agents dressed as Brentwood PD and BPD paddy wagon officers and a BPD paddy wagon and a dark building off the grid to do the interrogation. She told me sure she could arrange that.

That in fact there was an abandoned building twenty miles outside of town that all the town folks have forgot about. It would be perfect to do the interrogation there. It only needs a little cosmetic touch up to look like a BPD depot. She will have the things I need by the evening so we pull this off by the cover of night she said. I thank her and walked back to my office and told Albert of my plans we going to perform this evening.

Albert asked who would do the interrogation for Dominik knew who we were. I told him that we still have the face descrambler so we could dressed as BPD Detectives so he would never no who we are.

Albert said *"that's right we do I forgot all about that."*

I thought that would be best to pull him over for some minor traffic violation. Then our phony BPD officers would call for back up to do a drug search at the time the paddy wagon would show up and take him away for the interrogation. Albert and I went over the plans with the team that we had assembled so it could go off without a hitch.

We located Dominik car in the WBTS parking lot. The evening hours were at hand and we stationed agents near his location waiting to execute his pick up for interrogation. It was a warm summer evening and Dominik didn't know what he was in store this night!

Dominik got in his car and left the WBTS parking lot. Our agents posed as BPD officers followed at a safe distance to not be notice. They continued to follow him as he pulled onto Brentwood highway outer loop going toward the suburbs. We assumed he was going to visit his new friend Cecilia. We needed to intercept him before he reached the suburbs. Watching by monitors from the interrogation building I gave the order to the agents to engage our suspect.

Dominik was on the highway outer loop just minutes as the agents flashed their lights roar their sirens to pull him over. He came to a stop on the side shoulder thinking he was being pulled over by BPD officers. The officer walked up to his driver side door of his Aston Martin.

"License and registration please!" The agent said.

"What's the problem officer?" Dominik responded

"I said license and registration!" Says the officer to Dominik.

Taking the license and registration from him the agent pretended to look over them. Saying to Dominik, *"Do you know how fast you were going?"*

Dominik looking the officer in the eye said, *"The speed limit!"* He said this to get under the officer's skin for he felt that he hasn't done anything wrong.

The agent told Dominik that he was not driving the speed limit for the speed limit was fifty five mph and he was doing sixty two.

So Dominik said to the officer *"You pulled me over for seven mph over the limit! Really?"*

The officer told him to step out the car slowly.

Dominik thinking this was crazy asked the officer *"for what?"*

Responding the agent said *"I said step out the vehicle now"*, while placing his hand on his service pistol to show Dominik that he meant business.

When Dominik stepped out the Aston Martin he was told to place his hands on the roof of the vehicle and to spread his legs. The agent patted him down to see if he had anything on his person. Telling Dominik to stay there and keep his hands on the roof of his vehicle the agent walked over to his patrol car to call the paddy wagon to come pick him up.

The agent began to search Dominik vehicle to plant a phony illegal substance so they would have a phony reason to arrest him. Leaning over in Dominik car the agent pulled out of his shirt pocket a phony dime bag of an illegal substance so Dominik wouldn't see his plant it.

Seeing the officer pick up a small bag of a white substance from his floor board of his car, Dominik yelled, *"That's not mine! I don't know where you got that from but it isn't mine!"*

As the agent was executing the plan the paddy wagon arrived on the scene. The agent told him that he was under arrest. The agent began to read him his rights while placing handcuffs on him.

The paddy wagon officers took Dominik by the arm and led him to the back of the paddy wagon and place him in it. The team took Dominik and his vehicle to the interrogation site. Looking like a real BPD depot Dominik had no idea what was really going on. Placed in a dark room with just one spot light shining on him he set there alone for an hour to make him afraid of what was going to happen to him. Sitting in the room beads of sweat started to appear on his forehead.

Thoughts of going to prison and losing his job for something he haven't done made his nervous! Losing track of time minutes felt like hours to him. Unable to take the silence of the room he began to shout *"Do I get a phone call? I am supposed to get one phone call!"* He wanted to call Amber to tell her what was going on and see if she could contact her friend at the Brentwood Police Department to help him out of this mess that he was in.

The silence continued to make him sweat as if he was in a spa sauna. Roasting under the spot light made the situation worst! Finally after an hour of being alone in the room Albert and I dressed as BPD detectives with our face descrambler on enter the room. We told him the small drug charge was the least of his worries!

Confused of what we were speaking about he said, *"What are you talking about? I don't do drugs and that bag wasn't mine!*

That officer must have planted that stuff! And whatever else you are talking about I haven't done either!"

Albert said, "How do you know you haven't done it? For I haven't said what it was yet!

Puzzled of the whole situation Dominik said "Man what are you beating around the bush about? I know my rights and I won't say another word until I can speak to a lawyer!"

I said "Lawyer? You were not worried about a lawyer when you were breaking the law but now you want a lawyer! You criminals are all alike, you violate other person's rights but when you get caught you yell about you know your rights! What rights? You have rights if I say you have rights and I say you have no rights criminal scum!"

Being terrified Dominik scream that he wanted his lawyer; he was innocent of whatever we were talking about; he has not done anything he told the us.

Albert said as picking up a chair and throwing it against the wall to scare Dominik "You done it and you know we know you done it!"

Dominik with watery eyes of fear said "Done what? I know you know what? What are y'all pigs talking about?

I looked at Albert with a smile on my face. I could tell Albert knew that I want to laugh about how the interrogation was going. I walked over to the corner of the room to told Albert that he couldn't book an act half this good at Crowning Around.

Albert cracking a half smile saying to me "You have nothing on me! I kill! I shut the show down with my two gun act!"

I had to agree for he was part of the reason we were here tonight. His two gun act cause Dominik to know about him and I. I told him "You have me busing a gut in here! I laugh at you as much I laugh at Nicky Jones for being stuck in the 1950's."

Albert said to Dominik, "You are the prime suspect in home

invasion in a well to do neighborhood. You fit the description of the suspect that was seen fleeing the scene driving a dark color vehicle!"

Dominik seemed to be in deep thought, had a look on his face as if he has been caught with his hand in the cookie jar. Speaking to the Albert said, *"What neighborhood are you talking about? I am not only one in the town with a dark colored vehicle! A quarter of the town folks must drive a dark color vehicle these days."*

I asked him where he was on the day of BSU game shooting. Dominik answered, *"I was outside the stadium with my camera crew! We were reporting on the shooting! Speaking of shootings you need to find out who did all that shooting while you here picking on me about some home invasion I didn't commit!"*

So I ask him were he with his camera crew before the BSU shooting. And if he wasn't where was he at? Not looking me in the eyes he said *"I was inviting a friend at her place, we spent the afternoon together before I got the call from the news station.*

Thinking we had him where we wanted him for we can place him in the neighborhood and he just walked into our web!

Albert told him, *"The Westchester Heights neighborhood watch reported the suspect of a home invasion leaving their neighborhood about an half hour before the BSU shooting went down. So what neighborhood does the friend you were visiting live in again?*

Being flustered Dominik was red in the face as a mouse getting its limb caught in a mouse trap trying to get a piece of cheese to have a snack. For if he said his friend lives in Westchester Heights he knew he would place himself in the area of the invasion. So Albert asked him again of his whereabouts. Albert told him that his Aston Martin fits the description of the vehicle that was seen leaving that neighborhood. *"You need to go head come clean for we know you were in that neighborhood. We know your friend lives there and you were on your way there tonight! Your vehicle was spotted across the street from the house that was broke into!"* Albert said with an angry tone.

Dominik knowing he was caught but didn't want to fully admit to breaking in Josiah Lewis's house said, *"Yes my friend lives in the Westchester Heights, I met her a few weeks ago. I am the reporter for WTBS and my station wanted me to follow up on a news story. One night I was in Crowning Around, sitting at the bar I saw her so I struck up a conversation. I learned she lived in the neighborhood with the person that gave me a report of the news story. There no crime being in the same neighborhood. Because someone broke in a house when I was in that neighborhood doesn't mean I did it!"*

Slamming his fist on the table Albert told Dominik he was tired of the lies he was telling. Grabbing him by his collar pushed Dominik against the interrogation room wall. *"Now you going to tell me the truth! You broke into Josiah Lewis's home. Your friend is his next door neighbor and you broke in to his home looking anything that would link him to your story! You won't get out of this for you are going down for this crime."*

"We got your face on his security cameras and you finger prints all over the house." I said to trick him into a confession.

Getting tired of the interrogation for he has been drilled for hours Dominik said, *"How do yoy have my face on his security cameras and my finger prints all over his house for I wore a ski mask and gloves!"* Not knowing he just confessed to breaking Josiah's house he cracked a smile on his face thinking he out smarted the us.

I told him, *"Do you know you just confessed to the break in?"*

Dominik being a little out of it said *"When did I confess."* So I responded to him *"You just told us you wore a ski mask and gloves so how could have your face and finger prints. That's the confession"* I said.

"You jumped his fence and went to the back door and let yourself in and make your way to his home office. You ran sacked his office broke into his desk and made your way into his extended office room and cracked his safe. Once you got into the safe you helped

yourself to the important and priceless blueprint documents."

Fearing a lengthy prison time he admitted he stole the blueprints. He told the us that he didn't know what they were but they looked strange and they might be a linked to his story so he stole it. Albert asked him where he stashed the prints. To clear his conscious Dominik said the prints were in a storage unit he rents.

G.A.S knew they couldn't let him go back to his normal life like nothing has happen. National Security was more important than the well being of one person. They needed to brain wash him so he would forget what went on there that night. The fear that the brain washing wouldn't last and WTBS management would dig deep into what happen to him. The probability of the agency could be found out cause G.A.S to devise a plan to get Dominik Prince out of the country.

Pulling strings with their Pentagon contacts G.A.S had the Department of Immigration to cancel Dominik's visa. Not being a legal citizen of the United States of America, Immigration had him deported back to Ukraine. G.A.S recovered the stolen blueprints and having Dominik deported to his home country could put their full focus of the search of the Varldoion aliens.

Ploutcraft and Varldoionains have been elusive. G.A.S felt the BSU stadium attack was just the beginning of worse actions to come if they didn't find them in time to deliver the plans to help them with their own planet. It was of the most importance to stop an alien invasion from happening for Earth wasn't big enough for the Varldoionains and human beings.

CHAPTER 10

ONE FOR ALL AND ALL FOR LARKER!

Back on Varldoion Sho'aunor'es Ploutcraft gathers his crew together to devise a plan to get their revenge for the death of his 1st officer and lover Larker. *"The earthling will pay for killing my love!"* Ploutcraft said in his ancient Varldoion tongue. Upset about the death of Larker Ploutcraft felt the BSU stadium attack was the tip of the iceberg. He knew this attack would bring the Varldoion people one step closer to taking over the planet and making the human race their slaves.

Ploutcraft theorized if they attack the economy and military base of the super power country of the planet that would weaken the nations of the world. *"If the country they call United States of America falls this world will fall with it. They will say if America couldn't stand against the Varldoionains what chance do we have!"* Ploutcraft said to his officers. Going over the reports of his officers Ploutcraft saw there were two cities that they need to attack. The officers who did their studies of the eastern part of country told him that the economy center is a heavy populated town called New York City and their military control center is in a place called Washington, D.C.

Needing to study the human race close up and personal they will need to capture a large group to run tests on. The research would tell them what would be the limitations of the humans as slaves. They will use the slaves to build New Varldoion and make this planet suitable for them to live on over a long period of time. When Ploutcraft devised his plan to overtake the planet he had no idea that a small group of Varldoion-ains did this in the past in a third world South America Country.

Ploutcraft divided his crew into small groups. B'Elanna Linkasa and Ploutcraft with three officers and another group of four members would attack New York City. Ploutcraft put together two groups consisting of five members each. They would gather the humans that were needed to run the tests on. Varldoion Sho'aunor'es was equipped with weapons that could strike objects on the surface from space. The crew that stayed on the mother ship would attack the military control center in Washington D.C. from space.

Believing the trading post of the world flowed through the place called The World Trade Center Ploutcraft told his crew that they will destroy the world by stopping them from trading goods there. Ploutcraft said *"If you cut out the heart the body dies!"* He told them that they will burn that trading post to the ground and after they are done the only thing that would be left is ash. They needed a hot fire and this fire would take lots of fuel. They would start this fire at the top the towers of the trading post by dumping the fuel at its highest point and let it burn its way down the building. This would be done on both towers.

He told his Royal Guards that the humans have strange vehicles shape like giant bird creatures that fly and hold lots of fuel. We will take control of them and fly one into each of the trading post towers. *"We will destroy this post while killing many of these humans for Larker,"* Ploutcraft said. They been monitoring the flight patterns of the large aircrafts and notice that the large aircraft they needed came from large ports. If they used their mind control they could hide among the human beings and board the aircraft to hijack it. Because of their studies they knew that the crafts held a lot of humans at one given time. So if two groups flew the crafts into the towers the other two groups could capture the number of humans that they needed by hijacking two airplanes. Varldoion Sho'aunor'es could tracker beam the two aircrafts once each crew flew them close to Earth's upper atmosphere.

Reviewing their reports they saw the large ports near their targets were in Boston, Newark, and Washington D.C. Varldoion Sho'aunor'es equipped with a transporter could transport groups to Boston, Newark, and Washington, D.C. airports. With a flash of light the groups were transported to their required airports.

Ploutcraft and his crew used their minds to disguise themselves as humans and tricked the airlines ticket clerks to give them flight passes. Ploutcraft, B'Elanna Linkasa and three of his Royal Guards were at Logan International Airport in Boston waiting to board a flight to Los Angeles. Everyone who was waiting on American Airlines Flight 11 to board was at the gate. Ploutcraft, B'Elanna Linkasa and the Royal Guards were among the eighty one passengers in the waiting area for Flight 11.

The seventy six other passengers seemed excited about their long flight to Los Angeles as they talked and joked among themselves. Ploutcraft knowing what they were about to do and the passengers' excitement would turn into horror soon had a sense of pleasure in himself. Looking over at B'Elanna Linkasa said to her in a thought, *"Our hour of revenge will come soon."* She responded with a thought, *"They all will pay dearly Fearless Leader!"*

The voice of the gate attendant came over the loud speaker, *"American Airlines Flight 11 is now boarding First Class Passengers at Gate B32."* Ploutcraft and B'Elanna Linkasa boarded the plane with the other five first class passengers. The Gate Attendants boarded the remaining passengers and Royal Guards as their seat section came over the loud speaking.

All passengers, Ploutcraft and his Royal Guards were seated on the aircraft. The plane taxied away from Gate B32 early that Tuesday morning. The lead flight attendant began going over the correct aircraft procedures of what to do in case of an emergency. Ploutcraft said in a thought to his crew, *"They will have an emergency not long from now and none of this will save them from our wrath!"* Getting the okay the captain lined up the aircraft on the runway. The flight tower told the captain they were clear for takeoff. Moving down the runway strip the plane picked up speed.

The captain pulled back on the aircraft controls the plane began to get lift and take off the ground. Being in flight the craft climbed to cruising attitude. The captain made an announcement that plane was flying at thirty thousand feet and he will turn off the seat belt sign so they were free to move on the aircraft. Ploutcraft looked over to B'Elanna Linkasa who was in first class with him and said with his thoughts to his crew, *"Our hour has come to pay back these earthlings!"*

B'Elanna Linkasa being Ploutcraft ship's navigator had the knowledge to fly the plane to fulfill Ploutcraft's plan of revenge. Having his Varldoion short sword on him he jumped up and grabbed one of the passengers that was sitting in first class said, *"This is a hijacking so no one do anything funny like trying to be a hero!"* Saying this Ploutcraft stabbed the male passenger in the side and threw him back in his seat. Grabbing a flight attendant he yelled *"If any one of y'all tries to be a hero you will get what happen to this guy here!"*

Taking the flight attendant hostage Ploutcraft and B'Elanna Linkasa walked up to the cockpit door. Ploutcraft knocked on the door and demanded to be let in. *"If you don't let us in the cockpit we will kill every last member of your flight crew."* Being afraid for the lives of his crew the pilot gave the order to the co-pilot to unlock the cockpit door. As the co-pilot unlocked the door Ploutcraft rushed in and immediately stabbed the co-pilot who dropped to the floor like a sack of potatoes. Ploutcraft rushed over to the pilot and stabbed him. He threw the pilot to the cockpit floor. B'Elanna Linkasa sit in the pilot seat to navigate the aircraft. Ploutcraft took a seat where the co-pilot was sitting so he could supervise to make sure everything went as they had planned. Using his mind control on the flight attendant he made her go back and help his crew keep order over passengers.

Talking to his crew by using his thoughts Ploutcraft told them that the flight attendant he took hostage was under his control to help them keep the passengers in order so they could complete their mission. Thinking she was a part of the hijackers the flight attendant walked up to the Ploutcraft's three Royal Guards and said, *"We have hijacked the plane as planned! Let us keep order back here so everything we planned will be fulfilled!"* The other flight attendants over hearing what she had just said wondered how she being their friend and co-worker for years could betray them.

Meanwhile in coach a few of the passengers began to talk quietly among themselves. *"What is going on?"*

"Did they just kill someone in first class?"

"Don't talk so loud for we don't want them to come back here and try to harm us."

"We need to do something; we have no idea what they are planning to do."

"Yea but you heard what they said don't anyone try and be a hero. I don't want to end up like that guy in first class that was stabbed for no reason!"

"I understand but if we don't do something we will all end up like that guy one way or another. I have a feeling this won't end good if we do nothing!"

In the cockpit B'Elanna Linkasa took control of the plane and changed its course from Las Angeles to New York City.

Ploutcraft looked over at B'Elanna Linkasa and said, "*Now we shall get our revenge on The United States of America.*"

One of the passengers that were in coach said to the others "*I can't wait any longer; we need to do something and do something now. I believe we are not flying to LA any longer. And who knows where they are flying too or what they will do with us? For if we die I rather die fighting!*"

Another passenger spoke up and said "*You heard what they said no one try and be a hero. So why are you trying to get all of us killed? You don't know when they get to where they are going too that they just won't let us all go free.*"

"*If they were going to let all of us go free why hijacked a plane with hostages? And if they just wanted to fly somewhere, why not just rent a plane and fly there? I feel they have some evil plans and it don't include us being alive when their plans are complete. So we need to do something now if we all want to stay alive!!*"

"*I will jump on one of the hijackers when he walks back here.*" One of the three Royal Guards saw some of the passenger in the back of the plane talking to one another so he went to the back of the plane to stop them from talking. The passenger who wanted to attack the hijacker leaped out of his seat as the Royal Guard walked past him. He jumped onto his back, startled that someone had the guts to defy them he quickly reacted by throwing him to the floor and to make an example of him he stabbed him in the stomach with his dagger. "*I told you all not to be any heroes, see what trying to be a hero gets you!*" The passenger was left lying in the floor of the aircraft bleeding.

"*I told him not to try anything but he would not listen to me. All he did was get himself stabbed and has the hijackers real upset. Now he will bleed to death! Why did you have to try anything, I told you not too. Why didn't you just listen to me?*"

B'Elanna Linkasa said to Ploutcraft, "*We are close to our target, just about twenty miles off from our strike.*" Their plans of crashing the huge Boeing 767 into The World Trade Center were being fulfilled. There wasn't a thing in their way to stop them. G.A.S didn't know that Ploutcraft and his Royal Guards had hijacked four airplanes, and planned to crash two of those planes into The World Trade Center.

American Airlines Flight 11 was making a bee line straight for WTC North Tower. Minutes from flying into the North Tower Ploutcraft told his Royal Guards to come to first class section of the plane and be prepared to be transported back onto Varldoion Sho'aunor'es. Ploutcraft knew the plane was full of fuel and it would make a hot mess in the North Tower. Giving the order to the crew on Varldoion Sho'aunor'es Ploutcraft, B'Elanna Linkasa and the three Royal Guards were transport onto the mother ship. As they were being transported there was a flash of light and the plane crashed into the North Tower. The plane crashing into the side of the building caused the fuel to ignite. There was a great explosion and a huge hot fire began to engulf the top half the North Tower of the World Trade Center.

Around the same time as American Airlines Flight 11 was being hijacked by Ploutcraft, his Royal Guards were hijacking United Airlines Flight 175, United Airlines Flight 93, and American Airlines Flight 77. Just as American Airlines Flight 11 crashed in the side of the North Tower the crowd on the street stood there in total shock. Wondering what had just happen, people began to yell *"a plane just flew into a building!"* *"That's the North Tower of the WTC and it was stuck by a big plane!"* The crowds flooded the streets of Lower Manhattan to see the black smoke come from the WTC North Tower cause by the fire that was burning uncontrollable.

Not moments after New Yorkers watched in horror the burning of the North Tower, The Royal Guards Crew on United Airlines Flight 175 did as Ploutcraft did with his plane and bolted like lighting into the WTC South Tower. Not one but both tower had been struck by airplanes before 9:30 A.M. Tuesday September 11. The crowd was caught by surprise when the first tower was struck but when the second tower became victimized as the first the crowd was dumbfounded. Not knowing what to do they watch in horror.

Ploutcraft's other crews hijacked United Airlines Flight 93 and American Airlines Flight 77. They flew these planes to the mother ship as planned to run test on the passengers. Ploutcraft order the crew on board the Varldoion Sho'aunor'es to fire a laser beam at The Pentagon. Ploutcraft aimed to get revenge for the death of Larker. He wanted the Americans to pay for they did to his ship mate and lover. Blinded by rage he pushed the main mission aside to get his revenge. Receiving Ploutcraft's order they fire a laser beam that struck The Pentagon which killer hundreds of military personnel. Varldoion Sho'aunor'es tracker beamed United Airlines Flight 93 and American Airlines Flight 77 onto the ship. As the planes were being pulled out of earth's atmosphere the force of the tracker beam and earth's atmosphere pulling against each other broke off the planes' wings and engines parts causing them to fall in a open field.

The World Trade Center attacks and The Pentagon shooting and the down aircrafts parts in the open field caught the attention of the whole country. Ploutcraft well planned attack went off without a hitch. Striking the first blow Ploutcraft could sit back and revel in the carnage of the thousands of Americans lives he took this day for Larker. He told his crew to start to test and study the humans. If they were going to invade and conquer the earth they needed to know every strength and weakness of the humans.

The day seemed so unbelievable to the country. The public had no understanding what had happen. But The President called his military counsel together to get intelligence. One of the leaders told The President that they had agencies on the case to know the truth of the actions that happen. The President wanted to be informed on the findings as soon as possible. The President called a press conference to tell the public that they are investigating the acts of violence. They had no need of worry for these acts of terror will be paid backed in full to whoever caused them.

G.A.S was monitoring the attacks for they had the MO of the BSU attack. The government leaders put G.A.S on the case to get to the bottom of the events of terror.

ALIENS, TERRORIST, AND SECRETS

Receiving the orders to meet at G.A.S. headquarters I hopped in the Cavalry Cross to pick up Albert to go to base. We watched the news of the hijackings, Albert began to voice his opinions of what he thought had happen. We had a little debate if the hijackings were related to the BSU stadium shooting. We went over the details of the BSU shooting to see if the modus operandi fit what we knew of the plane hijackings.

We knew the shootings were performed by people that the aliens used mind control on, and we told the public that they were terrorists. Not knowing if the hijackers were under any mind control but when we knew the terrorist involvement was what the government came up with so the public would not have knowledge of aliens. So if the government says it was terrorist it was alien involvement. Albert and I discussed this all the way to GAS 225.

Waving at Nicky Jones we pulled into the garage and went to GAS 225 parking lot. After we parked we walked into the building and went straight to the conference room. The whole G.A.S staff personnel were in the huge conference room waiting for the start of the briefing with Director Beck. With a serious look on her face Director Beck got straight to business. *"We all seen the news and heard the terror of this day. But unlike the rest of the country we know who is the cause of all this horror,"*

I said to Director Beck, *"Albert and I were discussing on the way to base that the WTC crashes and BSU shootings were the way for the aliens to get back at us for the killing of their female alien mate."*

She said *"That may be the case, we need to get to New York and Washington asap. The Secretary of Defense has assign G.A.S. To do the investigation, we will be disguised as FBI agents and all other agencies will be kept from the scene for national security while we investigate."*

Albert spoke up saying, *"The world will be watching with twenty four news coverage not just Brentwood news. National news crews will be filming our every move."*

So I said *"If we set up a large perimeter so their news cameras cant get a good shot of the site and restrict a no fly zone so the news choppers cant fly over to see the area to get footage stating public safety after the jackings, we will be fine."*

Director Beck responded, *"Yes all the footage they have is of WTC Towers attacks which was a short footage of two planes flying into WTC North and South Towers. The camera footage of the laser beam from space shooting the Pentagon taking from across the street, we have that in our procession. No one will see this footage but us."* Haven't seen the footage I asked if it could be played in the meeting. She allowed the staff to view it.

Director Beck handed out the assignments to the staff, we had a military style jumbo jet waiting on the base runway for our departure fill with the equipment we needed for the investigate. I took a few weeks leave for my classes stating I needed to take care of some personal business out of town. After the meeting I called Monica to inform her that I had to go out of town for a few weeks to New York for a military consulting trip. Having our bags packed we all loaded onto the jumbo jet heading to NYC.

The flight to NYC was quick for there were no time to waste. As we landed Monica sent me a text that her and the boys were going home to visit her parents. The Trade Center has them a little a shook up for they were planning to take a trip there that morning to visit an investment broker but something told them not to go there. I was a little blown away that an angel was looking over them and kept them out this whole mess between G.A.S. and the aliens. I text her back saying be safe, I miss her and I'm thinking about her.

Arriving at the WTC site the National Guard had blocked off a 10 block perimeter like we requested to keep the news crews from seeing the site. Disguised as FBI bomb investigators field agents we collected all the data that was left behind by the aliens. There hundreds of local and national news crews on the site wondering what was going on and who has cause this destruction.

The nation waiting on a word from the President to give official word from the White House. The President spoke to the nation an hour after we arrived on the site to address the terror. "We will strike back at the person or persons who were the cause of so many American life. The nation has started it's investigation and what has happen was a terrorist attack on American soil. There will be a official report after the investigation was completed. The rescue effect has started to save survivors." He told the nation.

Albert walked the ruins with his hand held Video Eye In The Sky that was linked to a top secret military satellite that could play back footage up to 24 hours of a location. Albert scan the area that he want the footage of and download that to lab van that was on site. Awesome Blossum and few other agents were assigned to investigate the airports where the hijackings took place. They walked the airports with the Video Eye In The Sky and downloaded their footage to the lab van at WTC. After collecting the physical evident and the video footage we turned the site over to the rescue crews.

Tom and James worked in the lab van to view the evidents that were collected. The airports where the hijackings took place and WTC North and South towers were full of Eos Asta (an alien rubber like material). This physical evidents alone show that the aliens were involved in the hijackings and WTC plane crashes. There were no physical bodies of any aliens at the scene, so we don't know if the mind controlled people to do the hijackings or not until we can watch the video eye in the sky footages and pull all the details together. We didn't believe that Ploutcraft and the Varldoionains were the type to be suicide bombers. We were not sure of the range of their mind control ability but we are sure they won't kill themselves to kill someone else.

Tom and James saw the footage from Logan International Airport in Boston, Massachusetts showed that the alien from Agent Blossum's sketch was present at that airport . He was there with another female alien and three other male aliens. Tom called Albert and I over and said *"y'all need to come see this!"* So we went into the van to view the video that they had. To my shock I saw the alien from Awesome's sketch. When they called the first class passengers he and an unknown female alien walked onto the aircraft to sit in first class. The other three aliens boarded the plane to sit in the middle section of the airplane. Now we are sure that Ploutcraft and the Varldoionains were the hijackers. Now we need to discover how they got off the planes before they crashed in WTC towers.

When they view the WTC tower crash video the film showed a flash just before the planes crashed into the buildings.

James asked, *"What is that flash of light?"* They played it in slow motion and couldn't figure out what that was.

I said I know what that flash is for I seen it before.

Tom said, *"Really, what is it?"*

I said *"Yes, when we use the transporter in SUV it makes that flash. So Ploutcraft and the Varldoionains were being transported from the aircraft before it crashed, that is advance tech. Our transporter only transport packages not living beings! Tom y'all need to get your hands on that so we don't have to do all this driving and flying all over place! It would cut down on travel time! Ha Ha Ha!"*

James laughed and said, "Josiah, *you must want your feet where your hands are and your hands where your feet are! Ha ha ha!"*

Albert looked at me and said *"Y'all ever looked at his hands it might be an improvement! Ha ha ha!"*

So I laughed at Al's joke and said *"Whatever Al! Like your hands look any better than my feet! Ha ha ha! Y'all know we military men have poor looking hands for we are hard working men!"*

They all shook their heads and said you are right. So I told them lets get back at the task at hand and find Ploutcraft. We drove to the fake FBI base that the Secretary of Defense had arrange for our arrive. Tom and James put together the video footage of the airports of all the aliens and of WTC crashings. The airport footage showed two planes being hijacked and being tracker beamed in to out-space. The footage doesn't show a mother ship but it shows the location where the planes disappeared.

Arranging the physical evidents and the video footage into a report they gave it to Director Beck. She called an all staff meeting after viewing the report, We knew that Ploutcraft's mother ship had a invisible cloak, now we have a good idea where in earth's orbit it was. She started the briefing by saying *"Good work people! I knew it was a reason why I pay you!"* The staff made a slight laugh because it was no laughing matter or that we were all up tight because of our military background either way we wouldn't let ourselves really laugh. She told us where we stood at this moment and stand by to hear our next orders.

With a minute to spare I text Monica to see how she was making out. She text me back and said that she just arrived at her parents home in Harlem. I told her I was at a military conference in Manhattan. If I get some free time maybe I visit her in Harlem and meet her parents. She text back and said that would be nice just let her know. I told her I would. I went to find Albert to discuss what was going on and to get his thoughts.

Nicole Beck set up a video conference with the high government security officials counsel at the Pentagon. Her briefing was faxed over to their Pentagon office. They were all shocked by what they read. Direct Beck said *"Yes the BSU attacks and WTC crashes were them getting back at us for shooting their female ship mate. That isn't the shocking thing, they took two plane full of passengers to there mother ship. We don't have an exact location of the mother ship but it is located somewhere Earth's orbit over Iraq!"*

Okay an official said. The President wanted to go to war with Iraq and now we tell him that Terrorists are supported by Iraq and started a war in Iraq to light up the night sky with our missiles to cover up that we are shooting into space to find their spacecraft. Director Beck said it was a good thing that we did the terror alert a few months ago so the people can believe that we need to go to war in Iraq to attack the terrorists of the WTC crashes. The officials said we were thinking ahead. Good work Director thank you staff for their hard work. Stay at the fake FBT base in Manhattan for now for we may have more assignment for you soon. We contact you in a next few days to inform you on where we stand. Director Beck said that G.A.S will await their next order and closed out her video conference.

The next morning she called an all staff briefing to inform us on the situation at hand. She greeted us *"Team the government security counsel will tell the President that terrorists are being supported by Iraq and they will advise him to go to war with*

Iraq so they can cover up shooting missiles in the Iraq night sky to discover the location of the alien's mother ship."

Al looked me and said *"that's a major cover up a whole war with a country that has nothing to do with this situation ."*

I looked back at him and said *"Yeah, it seems that's what our government does these days to keep national security."*

He responded by saying *"Hey will they let me go over there and shoot my big guns!"*

I smiled, *"That's what got us in all this mess your two big guns! Ha ha ha!"*

Seeing us talking during her briefing Director Beck asked, *"Agent Lewis and Agent Crown do you two have something to say?"*

Answering I said *"No, Albert just was wondering if he could go to Iraq to shoot his big guns for he feels the need to shoot something!"*

"Agent Crown you haven't got enough of shooting something? What if we tell the alien we give them the person that shot their mate and leave the rest of us alone?" She laugh as she said it.

The room laughed along with her. I said *"exactly! Ha ha ha!"* Al not liking the room laughing at what she spoke said to me *"Jo you should be thanking me for I didn't let them shoot you new Baby or did you forget she was in the club? We could have traded your female for the female alien that's up to you! Ha ha ha!* The room and Director Beck laughed along with him. I didn't think that was all that funny but he just got me back for throwing him under the bus with Director Beck so there was nothing I could say but sit there and take it.

It was not long after our briefing that the President held his national press conference to address the nation about his plans to go to war with Iraq to strike back at terrorists for their attack on American soil. Though the President wasn't aware of the true situation at hand he explain to the public the knowledge he was told by his cabinet. The cover up was on and Congress has approved his war in Iraq.

The US armed forces invaded Iraq. Starting with night strikes that lite up the sky like a 4th of July fireworks show. Some of G.A.S top personnel staff, which Albert and I was a part of, were station at a top secret Middle East military base. It felt like my US Marines days all over again. Tom inputted the location of the passenger aircrafts disappearance into the missile computer. Albert asked for the honor of shooting the missile for it has been months since he has got to shoot something and the missiles were bigger than his guns.

Gun ho, with a smile Albert pushed the button to fire the missile. With a crack the missiles left the surface like an Apollo 13 rocket. They climbed up in the night's atmosphere and left the horizon with it was a lunar launch. All of a sudden there was a crackle and a big bang and no one but us notice the difference between our missiles crackle and bang and the US armed forces fireworks show. As we aimed our telescope in the direction of the bang a large triangle shape ship appeared in Earth's orbit.

Albert yelled *"Man I am good! What would y'all do without me? On the first shot I got them."*

Laughing I said *"Al don't get all ahead of yourself! All you did was push a button. Tom did the hard work by typing the data in to the computer!"*

Agreeing by shaking his head Tom said *"Yea Al! I did all the work."*

"The button wasn't easy to push it tried to fight back but I force it down! Ha ha ha!" Albert said.

I told them all jokes aside our missiles striking their ship, they probably felt this was the start of a war to them. Though we all knew the war started when they blow up the trade center towers with those planes. We could except for them to fight back with a strong force. We didn't know what type of high advance weapons they may have. We wanted to handle the situation in a peaceful manner but all that went out the window when so many American lives were lost. We felt that this was our planet our land our home and no being from another planet will come here and take it from us.

Our satellite caught an image of a laser ray blowing up a US Marine tank. It happen so fast that the Marines thought the tank ran over an Iraqi land mine. Seeing this Albert wanted to take control of a drone to fight back. Suddenly the earth shook under our feet. Albert said, *"No one told us that they have earthquakes here!"* Looking at him I responded, *"I don't think that was an earthquake. My best guess would be that spaceship track the location of our missiles launch and fired back at us."* With anger in his voice Albert yelled *"Hell Nah, it's on now! The bastards want some come get some! Somebody hand me my two Widow Makers I will finish this before it get started!"*

I spoke to Albert lets patrol the grounds of the base to see if anything was going on. He agreed so grabbing his Widow Makers and followed me outside. All of a sudden there was another shake. Falling to the ground I saw a flash of light and a being appeared out of thin air. I called Albert on the headset. *"Hey Al are you seeing what I am seeing?"* Responding back *"I don't know Jo what are you seeing? I see these strange aliens popping up all around the place out of nowhere."* I told him that I was seeing the same thing.

Picking myself up from the ground I saw the alien that was in Crowning Around. Saying to myself this must be Ploutcraft. Calling Al, *"Your friend from the club is here!"*

He responded, *"Huh? I thought she was dead on ice in the lab at the base! What's she doing here?"*

Laughing at his train of thought, *"Not her, the other one! The male!"* I said.

"Oh him I forgot he was still out there for a second! My bad! So you see

him now?" He said.

"Yes he is running straight at me. He looks a little angry. You shoot his mate and his ship and he is angry at me go figure!"

"Yeah we all probably look all the same to them!" Al said while holding back the tears of laughter.

While I was getting the words, *"This isn't a laughing matter,"* out my mouth the alien Ploutcraft who was running toward me leaped in the air to land on me with a elbow drop like we were in a wrestling match. I dodged his advance. Not knowing he could speak English he said *"You earthlings think you can shoot at my ship Varldoion Sho'aunor'es and we wouldn't fight back!"* Shocked by what I just heard all I could do is stare in amazement. I just hear a space alien speak and it was in English and clear enough I could understand it all. At this moment I kind of wish I had Al's two big mighty guns. I was trained for hand to hand combat in the marines but as a pilot I never had to use it until now.

I told it that they will not come here and try to take over our planet and we won't fight to do something about it. They need to go find another planet to take over. Ploutcraft look on his face seemed to be puzzled of why his mind control ability would not work on us G.A.S agents. I wasn't about to let him on our little secret.

Then he said *"All you earthlings will pay for the death of my lover and ship mate Larker!"*

"Yeah she on ice like you all will be if you don't get back on your ship and go back home to your home planet! We drew up blueprints to help save your planet but because your actions we don't really care what happens to your planet!" With a loud voice I yelled.

Then he leaped up in the air and flew toward me. What? I said to myself he can fly. Someone wake me up from this nightmare I thought. This isn't fair no one told me they could fly.

I raised my Sleep Maker 2000 and grabbed it with both hands pulled the trigger. The blast hit him in the chest and knocked him on his back.

I said to Al, *"You know they can fly?"*

He responded, *"No! I haven't seen any aliens flying! I shot two! Woo Hoo! Finally I got to shoot something and not get in trouble for it! One was like rubber, Stretch Armstrong but he was no match for my widow makers! Tom did you bring your bags and toe tags? I am going to have a few extras for you and the boys and girls to study back at the Lab!"*

As Albert was talking to me about his widow makers Ploutcraft leap of the ground with force as if he was MJ going for a mighty tomahawk dunk. His fists stoke me on the top of my head. I went down to one knee, he grabbed me by my throat with one hand and lifted me off the ground and my feet was swinging in the air. I yelled *"What The Hell!"* He hit me with an uppercut that knock the wind out of me for a minute or two.

Getting my thoughts back together, this alien doesn't know that we marines are trained killers. Breaking his grip on my throat, having my balance back with my feet on the ground I threw my own uppercut that connected to his chin that rocked him back onto his heels. We were about to be Smoking Joe and Ali out here! And when I done with him there won't be enough of him left for a second fight.

I bobbed and weaved like I had the quickness of Sugar and connected with the power of the Greatest of all time. Punch after punch and blow after blow he kept coming forward to fight toe to toe. He hit me with a wild haymaker that knocked on my butt. He caught me with a lucky shot but I wasn't going to take a TKO from him in this fight. I wished I could get a standing eight count but this was a street fight not boxing. In a street fight or desert fight, for we wasn't really in the street, anything goes.

He grabbed a large stone to smash my head with while I

was laying on my back from that wild haymaker. As he raised the large stone over his head I reach for the widow maker that Al toss my way when he saw I got knocked on my backside. *"Jo you need some help over there? Stop playing tag with that Damn Alien and kill him already!"* I shot once in his chest that rocked him backwards and another in the head that put him down for good. I walked over to Ploutcraft to see if he was still alive. He did appear to be dead I told Albert for he wasn't moving. When Ploutcraft fell the Varldoionains quit the fighting. Having no leader they were no longer interested in a war that they couldn't win with just a few star fleet crew members. Setting course to worlds unknown they left earth's orbit.

Tom ordered his crew to bag and tag the remains of the aliens. James reported that our satellites had indicated that Ploutcraft's spacecraft has left our solar system. Al hearing the news said *"If you can't stand the heat then stay out the kitchen."* Looking at him I started to laugh for I knew everything he said he could back up. Al was a silly guy but he was as tough as they come too. If they decide to return we would be ready for them this time.

The President had his war in Iraq, the alien had left the planet and no one knew the truth of what had happen so our cover up would continue. G.A..S left the Middle East and return to Manhattan for a debriefing. Director Beck thanked us all on a job well done. She told us that the nation was safe once again. Our government called us in secret to do a mission and we perform like the stars that we are. Being pleased with the out come she gave everyone a few days of R and R.

I called Monica to see how she was doing. I told her that my conference was over and I had a few days before my flight left for Brentwood and I would love to meet up with her. She told me she was free and she would love to see me. I been looking forward to seeing her. The lasted time we were together seem to have been so long ago. Giving me her parents Harlem address

I arrived about ten minutes early just to get some extra time with her. Her father Charles Scott answered the door. I introducing myself I said *"Good Afternoon sir, I am Josiah Lewis, is Monica home?"*

"Come on in Josiah. Monica told us all about you. I am her father Charles Scott but you can call me Chuck and This my wife Gloria. Have a sit, Monica will be down in a minute."

Sitting in the living room talking to Monica's parent I could see where she got her beauty from, for her mother was a beautiful woman. For it had been said if you want to know what a woman will look like when she is older just look at her mother. Monica walked in to the living room and stood beside her mother. They looked as if they could have been sisters not mother and daughter. We all talked for a few minutes before Monica and I went to get something to eat.

I never seen much of Harlem before so she decided to show me around after we ate. We stop at this little mom and pop diner that she loved. It had been there over forty years. I couldn't help myself for I was in love for when she looked at me I stared deep in to her eyes. She told me what happen to her husband hurt her a lot and it had been a long while since she been on a date. Her parent thought it was a great idea for her to date again and having a good guy in her life again she told me. But no pressure she told me while laughing and sipping her tea. I told her that it was no pressure for I was a great guy and I am here to stay.

After our meal we went to see some sights. We decided to take a walk in the park. We held hands and talked how we like each other. I didn't want this night to end but I was looking forward to many more to come. I was so happy for this beautiful woman I saw that day when I was coming out of my office I was now in a relationship with. I thought nothing could ever bring me down from cloud nine.

How was I so wrong! As we walked and talked this being appeared out of no where. Grabbing Monica as she screamed, the alien said *"You took my lover Ploutcraft from me so I will take your lover from you."* My happiness turn to sadness in a blink of a eye. I said this couldn't be the dead female alien that Albert shot in his comedy club but it looks just like her. I believe Ploutcraft called her Larker. I said *"Larker let Monica go this between you and I. She has nothing to do with this."*

Larker responded, *"Just like you earthlings cut me open and ran your little text on me some shall I do to her. Don't worry you shall get her back a piece at a time. Lets see if all the kings men and the kings horses put this egg back together again?"*

"You won't do anything to the woman I love!"

As I was speaking it made a loud yell that blew me into a tree in the park. When I came too Larker and Monica was gone with no trace of where they had gone too. I called Albert to inform him on what had happen. Calling G.A.S for we had a new mission to stop this new terror that threaten not just me but all of us when we live and our love ones. I vowed to get Monica back alive if it was the last thing I do!

THE END

www.ingramcontent.com/pod-product-compliance
Lightning Source LLC
Chambersburg PA
CBHW071242130626
46556CB00003B/1128